The TREASURE HUNT

The
TREASURE HUNT

ARMINÉ SANTOURIAN

XULON PRESS

Xulon Press
2301 Lucien Way #415
Maitland, FL 32751
407.339.4217
www.xulonpress.com

Paperback ISBN-13: 978-1-66282-861-4
Ebook ISBN-13: 978-1-66282-862-1

I dedicate this book to my grandmother and
only mother, Arminé Zita Varjabedian.
I did it, mama. I wrote my first book!

To my husband and best friend, Hrayr.
Thank you for believing in me
and making my dream of writing this book come true.

To my dear friend and editor, Alice Magner.
Thank you for being committed to our friendship,
By putting in hours of your time in making this book happen.

Matthew 10:29

"Are not two sparrows sold for a penny?
Yet not one of them will fall on the ground
outside your Father's care."

PROLOGUE

Endelman 1803

The King of Endelman was dead. His son, Prince Johann's coronation, was to be held in a week. However, rebels were planning a coup to replace the monarchy. There was much chaos throughout the country as the people heard rumors about a revolution. Prince Johann had inner turmoil between his responsibility to the throne and his desire to keep the peace in his country. If he took the throne, the rebels would use the monarchy as an excuse for an uprising. If he did the opposite, he would have betrayed his country and broken the oath he had made to his father.

When the king was on his deathbed, he asked prince Johann to promise him that his wife, Princess Antoinette, would adorn herself with royal ruby jewelry for his coronation. Prince Johann knew that his father was speaking of his father's jewelry for his mother, who died before they were completed. So, the Prince assured his father that it would be an honor to commemorate his mother at the coronation with that gesture.

Two days before the coronation, Prince Johann requested his wife to come to his chambers. "Come in, my soon-to-be Queen," Johann said.

Antoinette was wearing a gown made of the finest silk and endowed with pearls sewn into delicate lace when she walked into the room.

"Thank you, my soon-to-be king," Antoinette responded, then kissed Johann on his lips.

Johann took Antoinette's hand and asked her to join him on the balcony. A full moon lit the clear skies, and a canopy of star-like brilliance made for an enchanting evening.

"The stars are breathtaking tonight. It's the perfect touch for a perfect night." Antoinette said.

"My soon-to-be queen," Johann spoke.

"You are my Knight in shining armor," Antoinette responded, then kissed Johann's lips again.

"I have a surprise for you," Johann said tenderly.

"I love surprises!" Antoinette exclaimed, lighting up.

"Well, you will LOVE this one. Don't move. I will be right back." Johann responded.

Johann took out the jewelry, admired it, then took the necklace to the balcony. "Close your eyes," Johann said.

Antoinette shut her eyes and waited with anticipation. "Now turn around. No peeking." Johann requested.

With her eyes closed, Johann turned her to put on the jewelry around her neck. Johann covered Antoinette's neck with a perfect ruby necklace. Gorgeous sapphires and flawless diamonds formed the perfectly cut twelve-carat ruby that fell on her bosom.

"Open your hands," Johann said.

Antoinette held her hand out while Johann took out a matching set of long earrings, lay them in Antoinette's hand, and walked her to the mirror. Each earing was designed with a single flawless diamond surrounded by priceless Rubies and Sapphires.

"Now, open your eyes," Johann urged.

Antoinette opened her eyes to the most beautiful necklace and earrings she had ever seen.

"They are beautiful, and the gems are breathtaking," Antoinette said while touching her necklace and earrings.

"I am thrilled you like them; The set is not complete without this bracelet," Johann responded.

The luxurious bracelet had three rows of exquisite diamonds intertwined with sapphires, and rubies fit perfectly around Antoinette's dainty wrist.

Johann stood behind Antoinette and gently moved her hair off her neck. "You will be the most beautiful queen the world has ever seen," Johann said.

That night before prince Johann's coronation, he had a nightmare involving Antoinette: A faceless man approached Antoinette and threw her off the balcony while pulling her necklace off her neck.

Once Johann woke up, he immediately gathered his most trusted advisors, Felix, Mateo, and Liam. "I had a dream that Princess Antoinette was in grave danger.

"I want the jewelry destroyed before princess Antoinette realizes that they are missing," Johann said, frightened and visibly shaken.

The advisors were bewildered that the king had asked them to destroy what they considered the most dazzling pieces of jewelry. The artistry of the jewelry alone was enough reason to convince the king to change his mind.

"May I suggest another approach?" Felix asked Johann.

Johann had always trusted his advisors so much that he had considered them his closest friends. So, Johann took a deep breath to compose himself. "I am listening," Johann said.

"Are you prepared to share this vision with Princess Antoinette? I am concerned that she will question the absence of the jewels. What would you tell her?" Felix asked.

"You may have caused more damage than keeping her safe," Mateo warned.

"You would want to be honest with her," Liam echoed.

"A good night's sleep will give you a better perspective. If you still feel the same way tomorrow, then we will do as requested," Felix advised.

"I trust all your counsels. If you think that is what I should do, I will do as you suggest," Johann said.

"Before I leave, I have a few manifestoes I will need you to read and sign," Mateo mentioned, then lay the documents on the desk.

"Thank you all for sharing your wisdom," Johann said.

"Mateo, I will let you know when I finish reading over these documents," Johann replied. The three advisors bowed their heads in reverence to the king then left the room.

While reading the manifestos, Johann was distracted by a vision of three successive dreams. The King saw a scroll with names and their future genealogical order in the first dream. In the second dream, he saw himself writing a will to bequeath the Queen's jewelry to a woman named Anna Zigfield. Finally, in the third dream, he saw Anna recovering the jewelry. Though lasting a short while, these visions were seared in his mind, including all the names in the genealogy. He would write down the details of his visions after the coronation. But for now, his thoughts were focused on the coronation, Antoinette, and plans for the celebration. He decided that the soon-to-be queen should wear the jewelry as he promised his father.

An hour before Johann's coronation, he and his advisors came up with a plan to protect the queen while drawing out the Rebel.

During the coronation, the three advisors watched over the queen. While Johann and Antoinette were dancing, Felix and his wife danced with them. While Antoinette was mingling with her guests, Liam stayed close enough to the queen without the queen noticing him, and Mateo took on the role of casing the room searching for anyone suspicious.

Johann and Antoinette left the ballroom for a few moments alone when Mateo noticed a stranger looking down at them from the balcony nearby. Without a moment to spare, Mateo approached Johann and suggested that they go back to their guests. As soon as Johann had left with Antoinette, Mateo saw the Rebel looking in his direction then disappearing into the night.

The morning after the coronation, Johann awoke and spent the first part of the day praying and asking the Lord to guide the task xii | The TREASURE HUNT

revealed in his recent dream-like vision. The rest of the day was spent writing and putting into motion the plans that he would never see, but he would trust God to see them through.

CHAPTER
One

"But let all who take refuge in you rejoice;
let them ever sing for joy,
and spread your protection over them,
that those who love your name
may rejoice in you."
Psalms 5:11 ESV

Iranian Revolution 1979

The frigid January winds beat against windows, causing them to shriek. The wind picked up its pace as if it were trying to mask the random sound of gunshots. The curfew at sunset had left the city streets abandoned. Spontaneously soldiers shot their guns, claiming authority. The knowledge that they could strike at any time caused an unspoken fear in the city's inhabitants. A few weeks ago, the city court's first shootings to angry marches throughout Iran became a death trap for American residents.

According to the newscasters on television screens, America was responsible for years of Islamic oppression. A warning of hangings and imprisonments of traitors became a norm on the daily news.

Overnight, dust from the streets blew towards the base of the entrance stairs, hitting lady liberty's face. Once, she portrayed freedom. Today, through the revolution's irony, she became a betrayal monument. Many young men and women marched towards the American embassy, yelling, "Death to America." One of the young men pushed himself ahead to get to the building entrance, where his friends were waiting outside for him. Braham quickly opened the door, let his friends in, then secured the door with a crowbar.

Meanwhile

Across the street in an apartment, Anna spent the night with Katie helping her study for upcoming exams. Anna was an archeology intern at Shariz University under Professor Shahbazi. She was Austrian from birth and had been dedicated to historical work since she was a young girl. Anna's best friend Katie lived with her father and mother in an apartment across the street from the American Embassy. Katie's American father, who worked as a chef at the Embassy, spent most of his time planning, shopping, and executing meals for the staff and dignitaries who came and went. However, he left a note for Katie letting her know he was called in early to receive some deliveries at the Embassy kitchen.

Katie had been up at the crack of dawn after she heard her father leaving. She finished her chores and made Anna and herself breakfast when Anna awoke by the intoxicating aroma of rich coffee and fried bacon.

"Good morning, sleepyhead. I just put on a fresh cup of coffee for you." Katie chirped.

"Everything smells heavenly," Anna said.

Anna's eyes were puffy from being up helping Katie study all night, her long red hair was up in a messy bun, and her hands were tucked inside the front pocket of her oversized sweatshirt when she took her seat at the kitchen table.

"Here you go," Katie replied

Katie poured Anna a mug of steaming coffee then went back to cooking breakfast. Anna sipped her coffee and watched Katie break an egg over the pan.

"Fried or scrambled?" Katie asked.

"Scrambled. please." Anna answered.

Two slices of extra crispy bacon?" Katie asked.

"I would be crazy to say no to crispy bacon," Anna answered.

When Katie turned her back to Anna, she ate a strip of bacon.

"Hey, I saw that! Contrary to belief, I do have eyes at the back of my head," Katie chuckled.

Meanwhile

Braham and his friends had rounded up the Embassy staff and held them in a conference room. Braham paced the room carrying an Ak47 rifle over his shoulder. He walked by his hostages, who were blindfolded and paralyzed with fear. While Darius was guarding the entrance, Shahin watched Katie's father haul food supplies in the kitchen.

Meanwhile

Across the street from the Embassy, Anna was helping Katie dry the dishes. "Soooo... Do you want to be my partner in crime today?" Anna asked.

"No need to ask again. What 'cha got in that noggin of yours?" Katie asked.

"Let's ditch studying for a movie," Anna suggested.

"Let's do it," Katie agreed.

"First, you need to take a shower," Katie teased.

"Are you telling me I stink?" Anna asked, playing along.

"If it smells like a duck and sounds like a duck, it's a stinky duck," Katie said jokingly.

Anna gave a royal wave then sashayed herself to the bathroom.

Katie poured herself another cup of coffee, got comfortable on the couch then turned on the T.V. to watch the news.

"The Iranian Revolution has officially started. A mob of Iranian college students is spilling over the American Embassy walls." The reporter said.

"Dad!" Katie thought.

"According to recent news, hostages are being kept in the American Embassy. The reporter announced.

"Move out of the way!" a rioter yelled at the reporter.

The reporter moved closer to the camera.

"As you can see, the situation is escalating," The reporter said.

The Cameraman turned his camera on the students who were putting a match on the American flag. The flag broke into flames which caused the mob to cheer loudly.

"Wait. "The reporter said while pressing his finger against his earpiece.

"This just came in. we can confirm that the hostages are members of the staff. Stay tuned." The reporter replied.

Immediately after the Reporter had finished speaking, the mob celebrated.

It felt surreal to Katie when she watched the events unraveling before her eyes. The cameraman turned the camera to the men and women who marched the streets carrying signs and yelling. "Death to America!"

"This is bad, really bad," Katie said.

While Anna was finishing getting ready, she heard Katie talking to the TV.

"Are you watching a movie?" Anna called out from the bathroom.

"No," Katie answered.

"It sounded like you were watching one of your action movies," Anna said casually, then joined Katie on the couch.

"It might have been as well," Katie said quietly.

Anna took her seat next to Katie and watched the news in unbelief. She remembered that Katie had told her that her father had left to work early that morning. Anna's first thought was fearing for Katie's father's life.

"What was next?" Anna thought, then held Katie's hand.

Anna and Katie watched the cameraman press his finger on his earpiece.

"I just received news that the number of hostages has increased. I can confirm that more than 50 hostages are being held at gunpoint. Stay tuned as we bring you updates." the reporter said. The Cameraman pointed the camera to a group of men who were climbing over the embassy walls.

"I have to call my mom," Katie said, frantically then left to make her call.

Anna followed Katie to the kitchen, making sure her best friend would be all right, then listened to Katie speaking to her mother.

"But Mama, I know how to get in and out of the building without being seen," Katie insisted.

Katie listened to her mother speak. "Even with the smallest chance that I could be helping dad?" Katie said.

The mood in the room changed fast from calm to agitated as Katie continued to speak to her mother.

"Mama, I can't just sit here and wait while I know I can help dad," Katie insisted, speaking louder.

"Please wait." Katie's mother pleaded.

It became clear to Anna that Katie would not let anyone stop her from getting to her father, even if it meant putting her life in danger.

Anna walked over to Katie and patted her shoulder to get her attention.

"Tell your mom I will be calling my dad to see if he can help, Anna said gently.

"Anna thinks her dad might be able to help," Katie said calmly.

"How?" Katie's mother asked quietly.

"How can he help?" Katie asked Anna.

"He has done business with a few Iranian government officials," Anna explained.

Anna knew the chances that her father could help were slim. Still, she had to try.

"I am on my way home. We can come up with a plan when I get there," Katie's mother insisted.

"Honey, I love you," Katie's mother added.

"I love you too," Katie said and hung up the phone.

Anna picked up on Katie's new sense of urgency. "I know that look. You better not be thinking of doing something crazy without me." Anna said. "We need to talk," Anna said lovingly.

"I know you are scared. But you need to be smart about this." "So will I," Anna said.

Katie handed the phone to Anna. Anna called her father, Alford. Alford answered the phone before the first ring. Alford always had a keen sense when it came to Anna.

"Hi, honey. I was about to call you myself and ask if Katie's father was working in the embassy today," Alford said.

"Yes. Is there anything you can do to help?" Anna asked.

After Anna's mother had suffered eight miscarriages in five years, surgeons had told Alford and his wife she had what they called a hostile uterus and would not be able to carry a baby to full term. It was not until Anna was born that they understood how God could beat all odds.

"Honey, I would do anything for you but, this situation is too unstable for me to involve myself in," Alford said.

"What do I do? Katie is adamant about rescuing her father." Anna whispered.

"I can't wait anymore. I have to go." Katie interrupted.

"Wait!" Anna called out.

Anna's loyalty clouded her judgment when she decided not to let Katie go alone. Katie grabbed the spare keys to the apartment and ran out.

"I am sorry, Daddy, please understand I can't let Katie go by herself," Anna said and ran after Katie, dropping the receiver.

The girls headed down an alley across the street and up the rooftop through an adjoining building. Katie led Anna to the empty room where the air duct was.

"This is the way," Katie said.

Katie pointed to the chair in the room, suggesting they use it to climb into the duct.

"Here is the deal. I'll get into the air duct first, then help you up." Katie instructed.

"Okay," Anna said.

"I can do this for my dad," Katie convinced herself.

"Are you going to be all right?" Anna asked.

"I had not considered being smaller when I last climbed in these vents," Katie said.

"Let's do this instead. I'll go first and help you," Anna suggested.

"Thank you," Katie said, feeling tremendous relief.

Anna pushed herself into the duct's narrow neck then reached her hand out to help Katie up. Once Katie had climbed into the air duct, the metal groaned, and sun rays bounced off the steel walls guiding the way.

Katie stopped and tapped Anna's back, then motioned for them to stop and listen.

"Wait," Katie whispered.

Anna looked through the metal slats. "The hostages are in here," Anna whispered.

"Is my father with them?" Katie asked.

"I don't see him," Anna said.

"Let me look," Katie offered.

Anna moved out of the way for Katie to see.

Katie peeked through the vents when Braham's back obstructed her view. She intently listened and heard what sounded to her one of the captures speaking.

"Make yourselves comfortable no one is going anywhere for a long time," Braham said.

Anna turned to Katie and motioned them to keep going. After a few turns, Katie slowed down to a complete stop. "I think I heard my dad's voice," Katie whispered.

Katie peeked through the vents then looked up at Anna with disappointment. "That was wishful thinking," Katie said sadly.

"What now?" Anna asked.

"We have to get out here and walk the rest of the way," Katie said.

Before Anna and Katie made their next move, they stopped to make sure it was safe to climb out. Once they felt safe to leave, Anna reached out to Katie and held her hand.

"Are you ready?" Anna encouraged.

"Let's go get my dad," Katie said.

While Anna and Katie were walking towards the kitchen, Anna felt a sneeze coming on. The timing could not have been worse. Anna's eyes got watery, and her nose tickled. There was no stopping it now. Anna tried to muffle the sound by holding her mouth, but the sneeze erupted into a loud "Hatch! Choo!"

"I'm sorry," Anna whispered.

"It's okay. Let's keep going. Take a right." Katie whispered.

"Thanks," Anna said gratefully.

"Move faster. We do not have all day!" Shahin yelled at Katie's father.

"Did I just hear back talk?" Shahin yelled.

Katie's father knew better than to respond. Instead, he picked up another box.

"Did you hear me?" Shahin said snarkily.

"Halt!" Shahin screamed.

In the momentary silence, Shahin listened to what sounded to him as whispers. Walking into the kitchen, Braham immediately noticed Shahin visibly agitated. Braham quickly assessed the situation and released Shahin to go back to the hostages.

Anna and Katie heard footsteps walking down the hall along with the sound of doors opening and closing.

"Did you hear that?" Katie asked nervously.

The girls slipped into one of the rooms.

"Quick the closet," Anna whispered.

The girls held onto each other when they heard Shahin walking into the room and began silently praying. When Shahin drew closer, Anna and Katie started praying harder; Anna opened her eyes when she heard the doorknob turning. Katie took a deep breath and squeezed Anna's hand.

Meanwhile, Braham had seen Shahin walk down the hall.

"You are out of time, Shahin!" Braham yelled, startling Shahin.

"I could have sworn I heard voices," Shahin shouted.

"I could have sworn you were done looking," Braham said impatiently.

Shahin clicked the doorknob releasing the cylinder. Anna and Katie closed their eyes, anticipating the worst as the door began to open.

"It's an order!" Braham yelled at Shahin.

"Damn you!" Angry at Braham's order, Shahin slammed the door and then left the room. Anna and Katie waited until they were certain Shahin had left before opening the closet door.

"Now," Anna said.

As Shahin stomped away, his desire to prove himself right over-shadowed Braham's demand. When Shahin neared the kitchen, he changed his mind and went back to take another look in the room he was sure he had heard whispering. Braham became furious at Shahin for defying his orders. Without taking the time to think it through, he left Katie's father alone and went after Shahin.

Anna and Katie waited for Braham to leave before they entered the kitchen. As soon as Katie saw her father, she could not contain her excitement and yelled out to him. "Daddy!" Katie yelled as she ran to her father.

"Katie! What are you doing here?" Katie's father whispered, afraid for his daughter. Katie's father motioned them toward the exit.

"Let's go." Katie's father implored.

Dashing into the kitchen and pointing his gun at Katie's father, Shahin yelled, "Stop!"

Close behind Shahin was Braham. "Put that gun away, Shahin," Braham ordered,

Katie's father ignored Shahin and pushed Katie out the door. Shahin said with his gun still pointed at Katie's father, "If you don't want to die, you will stop now!" Shahin warned.

Braham tried to stop Shahin from shooting his gun, but the situation escalated too fast to keep up. Shahin shot his gun at Katie's father but missed. Katie ran out of the building as fast as possible, then hid behind a delivery van and waited for her father and Anna to come out. Hearing the gunshots, Anna watched empty shell cases rain onto the floor. Her heart pounded in her ears.

"Dad!" Katie yelled from outside the building.

Anna ran at full speed, trying to keep up with Katie's father while dodging bullets every step of the way. Katie's father barely got out the door before Braham stopped her progress by closing the exit door. Attempting to stop herself from running right into Braham, Anna's foot slipped from under her. Braham caught her fall and gripped her in a stronghold from getting away.

Shahin reloaded his gun, aiming it at Anna. In anticipation, Anna closed her eyes. She was not ready to die.

"I am dying today." Anna's voice echoed in her mind.

She closed her eyes as she felt a sense of peace envelop her. Anna experienced a sudden shift of perspective. The promise of Heaven filled her soul, and a picture appeared in her mind's eye of a sparrow sitting in a tree singing with his small and feathered neck raised into the heavens.

"God's eye is on the sparrow," Anna whispered to herself. She treasured in her heart her father's nickname for her, "My Little Sparrow."

"Put your gun down!" Braham yelled at Shahin.

Anna opened her eyes to behold her captors. As if he were a wild beast, Shahin was enraged at Braham.

"She is a liability. What is so special about this one? You are compromising the integrity of our cause!" Shahin yelled.

"We are not killing anyone. That is not what we agreed on. Now calm down and get a grip of yourself. "Go switch places with Dariush," Braham commanded.

Braham waited for Shahin to leave before he spoke to Anna.

"I will not hurt you, but I can't let you go either," Braham told Anna.

When Anna realized that Braham was her only chance of survival, she willingly joined the other hostages.

Anna stumbled into the room, almost tripping over one of the hostages. The hostage looked back at her and mumbled under his breath.

A man wearing a brown suit and sitting next to Anna wandered off in his thoughts. "If I had only stopped for coffee first." He pondered regretfully.

The man wearing a green Corduroy suit and sitting next to Anna was in his deep thoughts, "I almost missed the bus if only I had." he had hoped.

The woman wearing a blue dress was reflecting on her morning, "This is the morning I should have pushed the snooze button," the woman scolded herself.

The woman wearing a striped, blue suit, sitting across from Anna, reflected on her daughter and husband. "Did I give Emily her lunch money? The school will be calling Matthew when I do not show up to pick her up. He must be a wreck by now," the women panicked.

The woman wearing a green dress and sitting closest to the door pondered about her cat, "I hope the next-door neighbor realizes I never made it home and feeds Loo Loo. That cat is always hungry." the woman worried.

Anna found a corner spot in the room where she sat and watched the captors among the hostages.

As the day neared an end, hostages were taken one by one to use the bathrooms before nightfall. Anna was the first to go and the first to return and have the room to herself. In the room's silence, Anna felt the Holy Spirit nudge her and started to pray for Braham.

Anna had been too focused on her prayers to notice Braham sitting next to her and watching her pray. In the loneliness of the room, Braham felt drawn to Anna. She filled him with sweet memories of his life before tragedy stole his family. Memories flooded his mind.

The house had always smelled like his mother's cooking. The aroma of turmeric, garlic, and dill welcomed Braham to his favorite meal. Then, the smell of lavash fresh out of the oven, which his mother served with goat cheese and butter.

"It was a miracle that I did not become fat," Braham thought, chuckling in his mind.

Braham mostly missed his mother's encouraging notes that she used to leave for him. He recognized his mother's gentle spirit in Anna. He wondered if Anna would be willing to pray for him if he had asked her. Comforting thoughts of him and his mother praying together washed over him like cool summer rain.

"What's your name, little mouse?" Braham asked Anna. "

"Anna," she replied.

"Look at me," Braham said gently.

Anna lifted her head to see Braham.

"It's time to go," Braham whispered.

Anna could not help but notice a tenderness in Braham she had not seen before. He was gentle, even caring to the point that made her trust him.

"Leave now," Braham said.

"Please don't change," Anna felt compelled to say.

"It's too late for me. But not for you. You know the way out." Braham spoke.

Katie's and Anna's families quickly packed their belongings and flew to Austria in the next couple of days. With his government connections, Anna's father could get them a direct flight out of Iran to Austria, leaving behind the past and forging together toward a promising future.

CHAPTER
Two

"As soon as Judas took the bread,
Satan entered into him..."
John 13:27 NIV

Afghanistan 1960

B raham's father had fallen in love with the girl next door. It became mutual when they both committed themselves to marriage a few years after they had met. In time their love grew deeper and matured into an extension of their tenderness for their children.

Afghanistan 1972

Braham was thirteen years old when his mother was diagnosed with brain cancer, forcing him to grow faster by setting his life aside to become his mother's caregiver. In the months ahead, Braham and his mother grew closer and began confiding in each other. Braham's mother and Braham's relationship grew deeper after Braham turned his life to Jesus. When the time came closer for his mother to die, Braham found himself turning to Christ and finding comfort as his mother would have. Had it not been for his newfound faith, Braham would not have survived the upcoming years after his mother's death.

Braham leaned over to kiss his mother on her forehead before taking his seat by his mother's bedside. "Braham, is that you, my love?" Braham's mother asked.

"Yes, Maamaan," Braham responded.

Braham had noticed his mother losing her sight during carrying for her as she was getting sicker. come close." His mother said softly and tenderly touched his face.

Braham's mother felt for Braham's facial expressions.

"It's going to be all right, my son." His mother said.

"Maamaan, how can I say goodbye to you?" Braham asked.

"You can do all things through Jesus Christ who strengthens you." Braham's mother uttered.

"Philippians 4:19," Braham remembered.

"Yes." Braham's mother replied.

Braham got into bed with his mother, lifted his mother's frail body, lay her on his lap, and tenderly caressed her face. A pool of warm tears filled his eyes and slowly broke free. Braham's tears washed over his cheek as if the Lord was tenderly bathing his face.

"I'll save you a seat next to Jesus." Braham's mother spoke softly. Braham's mother took a shallow breath.

"My ... Bible..." Braham's mother said between breaths. Braham picked up his mother's Bible next to him.

"Deutero ... nomy 31:8." Braham's mother said.

"The Lord himself goes before you and will be with you; I will never leave nor forsake you. Do not be afraid or discouraged." Braham read out loud from the Bible.

Braham's mother asked him to come closer to her face and kissed him on his forehead for the last time.

"I love you, Maamaan," Braham said.

"It's only temporary." The Lord whispered into Braham's soul.

Afghanistan 1985

After Braham's mother died, Braham watched his father gradually becoming disillusioned. His father's inabilities to cope with his mother's death was the first step to his growing resentment for Braham and his twin sisters. Braham's father was withdrawn and absent from his children. He spent most of his time sleeping while Braham took care of his sisters. When his father was awake, he was angry and losing his temper. He was agitated with everything, especially when it came to attempting to care for his children.

When he saw they needed more attention, he became more agitated and angrier. He even started cursing God. Gradually darkness overcame his bitterness which made him unrecognizable. The gentle, loving man Braham had cherished memories with and looked up to his entire life became the source of his nightmares.

One day when Braham came home from school, he heard gunshots coming from the basement. He grabbed one of his father's guns, carefully opened the basement door, and walked down the stairs. It was not until Braham had gotten at the bottom of the stairs that he saw his father holding a gun and standing over his sisters' bodies. Sickened by what Braham witnessed and afraid of what his father would do next, Braham headed back up the stairs and ran.

"Get back here, boy!" Braham heard his father yell.

Braham's father's voice broke through Braham like a thunderbolt causing him to run faster and farther into the woods surrounding the village where he lived. Braham kept running and vowed not to look back. Ever. For days Braham wandered the streets in unfamiliar outskirts of town away from his neighborhood. He searched for a place to rest his head in and out of doorways.

After watching Braham's behaviors for a few days, an Iranian Shiite commander decided to recruit Braham and take him to Iran to join his Shia sect.

Braham kept his hands warm over the fire in the safety of his homeless comrades when the commander approached him with an offer.

"I can give you a better life." The commander said.

"How is that?" Braham asked.

"I can give you a family where you will be loved and respected," the commander answered.

"Why me? I have nothing to offer. Except this, and that's not enough." Braham explained, pointing at himself.

"Son, what I see in you is a man of integrity and strength. So much that I am willing to train you to be my successor," the commander promised.

The commander had been counting on Braham's vulnerability and cravings for affection and affirmation to mold him into his image. The commander had decided that before Braham could become the clay to his potter's wheel, he would first become the father figure Braham needed.

After several months of training, Braham had already exceeded the commander's expectations. The time had come for Braham to go on his first mission.

"I want you to take over this mission." The commander told Braham.

"Yes, sir," Braham responded.

"What have I taught you to say?" The commander asked.

"I am invincible. I am strong. I can do no wrong." Braham answered.

"In the name of Allah. Go." The commander said.

"Yes, sir," Braham said.

"All right, men, time to go," Braham announced.

The soldiers stacked the guns in the trunk then got into the white van.

Parviz soldered the last piece to his explosive gear, attached it around his waist, then met Braham at the van.

Even though Braham had known not to invest himself emotionally with his protégé Parviz, the young man had reminded him too much of himself.

Braham looked up from the trunk and noticed Parviz shaking uncontrollably.

"It is a privilege that Allah has chosen you to glorify his name," Braham said encouragingly.

"You can't afford to fail," Braham heard his commander speak in his mind. Braham looked into Parviz's eyes and saw his fearful eyes filled with tears.

"Soldier, what have I told you to say?" Braham asked Parviz.

"I am invincible. I am strong. I can do no wrong." Parviz answered.

"Now, get your composure back before the other soldiers see your weakness, then sit in the passenger seat. You are the guest of honor today." Braham said.

"Braham, in my office!" the commander called out.

Braham left his soldiers and walked to the commander's office.

"Yes, sir?" Braham asked after stepping into the office.

"What is the status?" The commander asked.

"We are ready to leave, sir," Braham said.

The commander left his office to see Braham off.

"How many targets today?" The commander asked Braham.

"The marketplace and the small village in Afghanistan," Braham answered.

"That should get their attention." The commander said.

"Yes, sir," Braham agreed.

"Make me proud." The commander proclaimed.

"Yes, sir. Let's go." Braham called out at the soldiers.

Braham tapped the back of the van, got into the driver's seat, and drove away with a large load of ammunition.

Once Braham reached his childhood village in Afghanistan, he turned off the engine and parked the van far enough away as not to be seen. Braham got out of the vehicle to let Parviz out and heard his mother speaking to him inside his mind.

"What happened to you?" Braham's mother asked in the crevasse of his mind.

"You left me," Braham answered.

Then he tuned out his mother's voice and opened the passenger's seat.

"You know what to do," Braham told Parviz.

Parviz nodded his head yes.

"In the name of Allah, go," Braham encouraged.

"In the name of Allah!" Parviz said, then started walking into the village.

"Wait here," Braham instructed the soldiers, then followed Parviz to the town.

When the villagers saw Parviz walking into the village court with explosives wrapped around his waist, they grabbed their children and ran into the fields. When a mother ran to get her two toddler girls, Braham heard his twin sisters crying out to him and begging for help. Braham wanted to yell at Parviz to abort, but it was too late. Braham watched in horror when Parviz pushed in the detonator in his hand and killed himself along with the mother and her two girls. While Braham watched in terror as the town burned, he envisioned his twin sisters lying in a pool of blood in his basement.

Braham hid behind a large rock and cried.

The pain of failing to save his sisters again was too much for Braham to shoulder on his own, causing his mind to shield itself by creating an alternative personality. As a result, Braham was no longer himself. Braham's training as a soldier had taught him to push past the emotion and not to feel, but the weight of the grief gripped him and messed with his mind.

The last thing Braham remembered was emerging from the ashes of his mind. He dusted the dust off his pants and discarded Braham's name. Instead, he chose the name Cyrus meaning conqueror, and drove off to join his Shiite brothers.

CHAPTER
Three

"Peace I leave with you; my peace I give you.
I do not give to you as the world gives."
John 14:27a NIV

Vienna 1987

Anna worked in Northern Africa on an archeological dig when she received a call from her mother telling her that her father had suddenly died from a cardiac arrest.

"Oh, I am sorry, sweetie, I forgot you were flying to Turkey to meet with your archeological team tomorrow." Anna's mother, Tanya, said.

"It's OK, Mom. I'll change my ticket," Anna responded.

Without hesitation, Anna put her grief and plans on hold for her mother.

"Mama, you are my only priority right now. I will be home as soon as I can," Anna said.

"Thank you, my darling," Tanya replied and hung up the phone.

Anna felt the accelerating engine in the belly of the plane that was flying her back home. She focused on the lines of the runway until they became a blur. Anna held on tightly to the armrest of her seat. A mouthful of rain clouds swallowed the plane as it adjusted its course, and raindrops blew past, streaking the window. The aircraft climbed above the dark and endless clouds. Anna felt her heart riddled with grief and a blanket of regret weighing her down.

"The doctors were worried about dad's heart. I should have known better than let dad cheat on his diet." Anna told herself.

Anna remembered what her father had told her in times like this.

"Guilt is a wasted emotion. It is the enemy of your soul. God knows your heart." Anna pondered her intentions.

"The truth is: Dad would have found another way to cheat on his diet. I had no control over his choices, I would never hurt him intentionally, and I loved him deeply."

"Cherish and protect the memories you and I have made together throughout our lives," Anna's father said, uttering in Anna's heart.

Anna sat back and closed her eyes.

"Thanks, Dad," Anna thought, then slept through the rest of the flight.

Details of the funeral service, from the plans to its execution was flawless.

Friends and family filled the small stained-glass church for Anna's father's memorial and burial service. The mahogany casket that sat in the middle of the church was covered with black lace and surrounded by flowers. A horse and carriage waited outside to take the coffin to its resting place.

Anna and Tanya took their seat next to the coffin, followed by the mourners. Once everyone had been seated, the visiting priest started his short service with an opening prayer.

While everyone's eyes were closed or looking down, Anna looked up and saw a line of people standing outside and hoping for a seat. She felt pride fill her heart when she realized the many lives her father had touched.

` After the service was over, the church bells rang, ushering the coffin driven by beautiful black horses pulling the carriage. Anna and Tanya walked somberly behind the casket.

After the ceremony, everyone was invited to the Zigfield villa for brunch.

When Anna made it to the villa, she saw Katie waiting for her. Anna had missed her best friend terribly.

Katie ran and gave Anna a big hug. "It was a beautiful funeral," Katie said.

"It was beautiful," Anna agreed.

Katie reached out and gave Anna another hug. "You don't call anymore," Anna teased.

"We talk once a week," Katie said.

"Well, it's simply not enough," Anna remarked and pretended to have taken offense.

"Once you stop pouting, I have some exciting news to share with you," Katie said.

"Let's go to the garden where we can talk in private," Anna suggested.

Anna and Katie sat on the bench and started catching up.

"Why did you not tell me that Randolph was attending Harvard University?" Katie asked.

"To be honest, it never crossed my mind. Why do you ask?" Anna questioned.

"Well..." Katie said, grinning from ear to ear.

"No... You and Randolph?" Anna guessed.

"I know. It just happened. We joined the same study group, then... we studied together, then... we went out for dinners then...." Katie shared.

"Then you guys fell in love," Anna concluded, grinning.

"Yes," Katie said and was about to burst into excitement.

"I am so happy for you. You and Randolph make a great couple." Anna responded.

"There is more!" Katie announced.

"I don't think my heart can handle anymore," Anna said, then broke into laughter.

"Ready for more excitement?" Katie asked.

"Bring it on," Anna answered.

"I got the internship I have been praying for," Katie said.

"You got the Paris internship," Anna said.

Katie and Anna jumped off the bench and squealed like little girls.

" I am so proud of you." Anna said, then plopped herself on the wooden bench.

"We have come a long way since Tehran," Katie replied.

"Yes, we have." Anna agreed.

The rest of the day, Anna and Katie spent their time helping Tanya visit with her guests.

The week after Anna's father's funeral, Katie left for Paris while Anna stayed close to her mother in Vienna by leasing an apartment. Anna's new apartment in the 1ˢᵗ district had easy access to her beloved Opera house, Wiener Staats Oper. The historical city was the backdrop of Anna's fondest memories with her father. Anna sat in her reading chair by the window and took a trip down memory lane.

Anna remembered being sixteen and wearing an evening dress and her distinguished father wearing his tuxedo and black tie. The night began with a dinner in a sophisticated restaurant on the famous Kartner Strasse and watching an Opera in the Commemorated Opera house. And then there was the time she was eighteen, and she and her parents had attended a wedding ceremony in the historical Saint Stephen's cathedral.

"I remember being a junior in college and going on an unforgettable trip to the Hofburg Imperial Palace with Dad. It was also the day dad told me of my royal heritage and some of the history of the Zigfield Villa." Anna said.

The painting of the King and his beloved family was a centerpiece in the villa's library. As Anna thought back to that painting, she was impressed with the signet ring's history and significance. The ring that her father had always worn and gifted her at his death was the same one King Johann had worn.

Anna stored these memories back in her heart then got dressed for another day.

CHAPTER
Four

"Each of you should use whatever gift you have received to serve others, as faithful stewards of God's grace in its various forms."
1 Peter 4:10 NIV

By the time Anna had turned the corner on her street, the cold winds had started, and the engorged clouds had burst into heavy rain. Large raindrops hit Anna's umbrella, and the wind billowed under the canopy. Lightning roared, flashing in the sky, forcing Anna to speed walk to her apartment building.

Anna opened the door, shook off the rain, and entered the building.

"What a night!" Anna announced to the stranger standing in front of the elevator next to the building manager.

"It's pouring out there." The building manager, Gertrude, said.

"I almost drowned out there!" Anna chuckled and head to the elevator.

As Anna was walking towards the elevator she realized the stranger was waiting for her.

"Excuse me," Anna told the stranger, then attempted to reach the up button.

The stranger moved to the side.

"Are you Anna Zigfield?" The stranger asked.

"Yes. Who's asking?" Anna questioned.

Without speaking, the stranger handed Anna a large Manilla envelope.

The stranger raised his eyebrows in a question with a quirky smile and then left the building.

"Waaaait!" Anna called out as he disappeared from the doorway.

"That was strange," Anna told Gertrude.

In the short time Anna had lived in the apartment, Gertrude had proven to be a trustworthy friend.

"I can't shake the feeling that once I open this envelope, there will be no turning back," Anna said.

"I know you have a curious nature, and you can't ignore it," Gertrude pointed out, then smiled.

Anna tore the sealed package open and took out three envelopes. Two of them were sealed in red wax with a familiar stamp. She recognized that the symbol bore the impression of the signet ring, the one belonging to King Johann, that her father had given her at his death. Excitement and a sense of mystery tingled up Anna's spine as she realized a profound connection with the contents of what she was about to read.

Anna returned the two letters with the seals to the manila envelope. Then she held up an official-looking letter with Müller and Son Law firm's letterhead.

Müller and Sons Law Firm Est. 1803

January 19, 1987

Dear Ms. Zigfield,

*Please read the contents of this envelope and call me
at your earliest suitability.*

Sincerely,

Heinrick Müller

Anna folded the letter and put it in the manila envelope with the two documents sealed with wax. "Everything okay?" Gertrude asked, looking at Anna's puzzled face.

"Hope so, but I'm not sure," Anna said.

"Do you need some company?" Gertrude asked.

"No. Thank you for asking." Anna answered.

"Have a good night, sweet girl," Gertrude said, then walked up the stairs to her apartment.

Anna stood there, not knowing how to respond. As Anna came to herself, she took the elevator to her apartment.

Entering her apartment, Anna put the manila envelope on a stack of mail. Feeling overwhelmed by the documents, Anna decided to reflect on these documents' magnitude before reading the contents.

Anna poured herself a glass of red wine and drew herself a bath. While Anna was soaking in the bathtub, she clearly understood King Johann folding his will, pouring red wax on the document, and pressing his signet ring into the wax. For a moment, Anna thought she had fallen asleep in the bathtub, but in reality, she had had a vision linking her future to King Johann from 1803. Anna got out of the bathtub and put on her pajamas, then hurried to the kitchen.

In great eagerness, Anna took out the two documents sealed with the signet, cracked the sealant, and began reading.

I, King Johann Zigfield, on this 5th day of November1803,acknowledgethisismylastwill andtestamentwithasoundmind.Ientrustthe rubynecklacewithamatchingbraceletandearrings, havingbelongedtoQueenAntoinettetothecareof AnnaZigfield,daughterofAlbertZigfieldthe second.Thesepiecesofjewelrywithflawlessgems weremadefortheQueentowearformycoronation. Thenecklaceisdesignedwithatwelve-caratruby surroundedbyflawlesssapphiresanddiamonds.The dropearringsaredesignedwithafive-caratdiamond surroundedbyrubiesanddiamonds.Thebraceletis designedwiththreerowsofgemsintertwined,one rowofdiamonds,onerowofsapphires,andonerow ofrubies.Thiscombinedjewelrycanbefoundby playinginatreasurehuntplannedoutforme.

Johann Alford Zigfield

Witnesses present:
Felix Müller
Mateo Wagner
Liam Zigfield

"A necklace, bracelet, and earrings? Anna thought.

Curious about the current value of her inheritance, Anna searched for answers in one of her books. "There you are." Anna said, then removed the book titled "The History of Currency."

Anna took out her calculator and read through the book until she found what she was searching then started doing the math.

"73,000,000 Gulden would equal 1,000,000 dollars in the year1803. Based on inflation, the jewelry in today's value is 20,000,000 dollars." Anna concluded then reread the will. "That is so much money," Anna concluded.

Before Anna put the will back in the manila envelope, she found another letter from King Johann. *"There is more to the story,"* Anna told herself, then broke the wax seal and read the second letter from the king.

Dearest Anna, November 7th, 1803

IamwritingyouthislettertoprotectourVillain ViennawhileRebelsseizedEngelman'spalace.You mayhavehadyourfirstvisionbynow,andthingsare hopefullystartingtomakemoresensetoyou.

Itallbegantheeveningbeforemycoronationday whenaspyfromagroupofRebelssawtheQueen wearingtheRoyaljewelrythatIhadgivenher thatnight.ThatwasalltheRebelshadneededto provethatIwouldrulelikemyfatherandcontinue oppressingthepeople.Amonthlater,Ihadavision ofaRebelkillingtheQueenandourchildren.

Aftermyvision,Iimmediatelygatheredmyfamily, abdicatedmyrule,fledwiththemtoourvillain Vienna.Wearelivinginrelativeobscurityandpeace atthismoment.DearbeautifulAnna,Ihaveonly seenaglimpseofyouinmyvision.IbelieveGodhas appointedyoutheheirtoamostsignificanttreasure.

Asmuchaswecanbesureofanythinginthislife,
IthinkGodhasgivenmepeacethatyouwillknow
whattodowithyourinheritanceandwhentodoit.
Ihaveinstructedmythreeclosestadvisorsonmy
plans.Theirheirswillbecomepartofthisquestthat
Ileaveforyou.Thejewelshavebeenhiddensafely
awayfromthosewhowanttodestroyourfamily.

Hereismyadvicetoyouasyoustartyourjourney.
LettheLordguideyouthroughyourvisions;no
mattertheobstaclesthatmaycomeyourway,donot
deviatefromthetruthandopenyourhearttonew
opportunities.

MayGodgiveyouthegracetoreceivetheblessing
that comes from Him.

Johann Zigfield.

Anna was stunned as she sat to process what she had just read.
She recalled one of the stories told by her father of a family heirloom
of rubies and diamonds that none of her recent ancestors knew,
whether it was fact or myth. Anna picked up the phone and dialed
her mother. While waiting for her mother to answer, Anna's mind

wandered in many directions. "Did Mama know about this?" "How much of this did Papa know?" "Is this even real?"

"Hello?" her mother asked. "Hi, mama," Anna said.

"Hi, sweetheart. Is everything okay?" Tanya asked.

"It will be. Do you have any time I can stop by today?" Anna questioned.

"I always have time for you," Tanya answered.

"Thanks, Mama. I am on my way." Anna said.

Anna took the tram to her mother's house then walked the short distance. By the time she had reached the villa, Tanya was waiting to greet her with open arms.

"Hi, honey. I made some hot cocoa. Let us sit in front of the fireplace." Tanya invited, then let Anna into the house.

"It is a cold but beautiful winter day," Tanya said.

"Hello, Miss." The maid, Cecelia said, then helped Anna with her coat.

"Oooh... it is chilly outside," Anna responded.

"You can get nice and cozy in the family room. I just added some new logs to the fire," Cecilia said.

"Thank you, Cecilia," Anna committed, then left to join her mother.

When Anna walked into the family room, Tanya had put aside a warm blanket and hot cocoa for her to enjoy. "I feel so loved," Anna said.

"You are. Now sit and talk to me. What is going on?" Tanya asked.

Anna covered her legs with the blanket, took a few sips of her hot cocoa, and took out the manila envelope from her bag. Her mother, observing Anna, noticed a mix of excitement and anxiety in Anna's demeanor. "Where do I begin?" Anna questioned.

"From the beginning." Tanya encouraged.

"As I arrived home today, a man I had never seen before handed me a manila envelope. Anna said.

While Anna was taking out the manila envelope from her bag, the doorbell rang.

"Cecilia, can you get the door?" Tanya called out.

Cecelia opened the door and retrieved an envelope on the door-step, then handed it to Tanya. Tanya glanced at the return address embossed on the envelope. It was from Müller and Sons Law Firm addressed to Tanya Zigfield.

"A letter from Müller and Sons Law firm similar to the one I was about to share with you," Anna said, surprised as she looked over her mom's shoulder.

Tanya smiled at that almost knowingly then read it aloud.

Müller and Sons Law Firm Est. 1803

January 19, 1987

Dear Mrs. Zigfield,

My name is Maximillian Müller. I am a member of the alliance King Johann established, a descendant of three of his most trusted advisors. Your husband was privy to our partnership and the purpose of it. I am writing you this letter to inform you that my son will be responsible for assisting your daughter, Anna Zigfield, in implementing King Johann Zigfield's Will, which was hand-delivered to Anna Zigfield's today 5:30 pm. In addition, my son, Heinrick, and I will be responsible for keeping you updated on Anna's quest should she choose to accept her inheritance.

If you have any further questions, please feel free to contact me at my law firm. Our alliance will remain intact until the completion of the implementation of King Johann's Will.

Sincerely,

Maximillian Müller

"Mama, why don't you look surprised?" Anna asked.

"I knew this day would come. If only your father were here to explain it." Tanya shared.

"Why did you not say anything?" Anna questioned.

"It was not up to me," Tanya answered.

"What about dad? He could have prepared me for this day. Knowing that I might be responsible for 20 million dollars worth of royal jewelry one day is a big deal." Anna said.

"That is why we did not tell you. It would have been too much for you to grasp. There is also the other side of the coin; dad had to consider," Tanya said.

"I am listening, Anna responded.

"He also had a letter King Johann had passed down to him, stating that your dad needed to wait till you turned twenty-five to tell you about his will. I wish your dad were here..." Tanya said.

"You are doing great explaining things," Anna encouraged.

"Thank you, honey," Tanya said.

"I have another question," Anna continued.

"Yes?" Tanya asked.

"Did dad have premonitions? I am asking because I think I had a vision of King Johann today." Anna said.

"Yes. I was the only one who knew about your father's premonitions." Tanya shared.

"Do you think these visions are from God?" Anna questioned.

"I do. Your father's visions resulted in the spiritual growth of the church." Tanya answered.

"His visions also saved you from possible harm." Tanya continued.

"Do you remember your dad coming home and telling you he changed his mind about you sleeping over?" Tanya questioned.

"I remember, Anna answered.

"He knew enough to stop you from making a big mistake that night," Tanya said.

"I remember her name was Heidi, and she was caught selling drugs that night," Anna recalled.

"God works in mysterious ways," Anna said.

"Yes, He does," Tanya agreed.

The rest of the evening, Anna enjoyed her mother's company by watching a Doris Day movie and having dinner with her.

After a restful night, Anna prepared a day and learned more about the King and his vision for her. Her new confidence had not come from her visions but from her faith in God. God knew what he was doing. She just needed to be trusting that this was the path for her life.

Early the following day,

"Müller and son associates. Maria speaking, how can I help you? The receptionist asked.

"I would like to speak to Heinrick Müller, please," Anna answered.

"One Moment, please, I'll connect you." The receptionist said.

"Hello, this is Heinrick Müller. How can I help you?" Heinrick questioned.

"My name is Anna Zigfield, and I am responding to your letter," Anna answered.

"Would you have time to get together tomorrow?" Heinrick asked.

"Yes," Anna responded.

"What about 9:00 am at Cafe Central?" Heinrick asked.

"That would work," Anna answered.

"How will I recognize you?" Heinrick questioned.

"I'll be the most beautiful lady wearing a red overcoat," Anna answered, feeling a bit of sass.

"I will be wearing a tan coat with a burgundy scarf," Heinrick chuckled.

"I'll see you tomorrow morning at nine," Anna said, then hung up the phone.

Heinrick put down his phone and went back to work.

While Heinrick was working, his administrator gave him a letter with a red wax seal. Heinrick broke the seal and began to read.

Place: The Men's Club

Attire: Formal

Time of event: 6:00pm

A car will be picking you up in front of the Staadtsopera at 5:00 Pm.

Heinrick took the tram to the fourth district and got off Ring Strasse, where he walked the rest of the way to the opera house. As soon as Heinrick arrived, a black limousine was waiting to take him to his new destination.

The chauffeur got out of the car and walked towards Heinrick. "May I see your invitation?" The chauffeur asked.

Heinrick took out the letter from his inside pocket and showed him his invitation.

"Thank you.'" The chauffeur said and opened the door for Heinrick. Heinrick got into the back seat and made himself comfortable.

"Sir, we have iced champagne, caviar, petite sliced pieces of toasted bread, and a cheese platter with grapes and figs for your enjoyment." The chauffeur said while driving.

"Thank you. I think I will have some." Heinrick said.

Heinrick poured himself a glass of Champagne, spread the caviar on a piece of bread, and placed some cheese and fruit on his plate.

"This is the life," Heinrick said, then sipped his champagne.

When the car stopped in front of the building, the Chauffeur let Heinrick out by opening the door for him.

"Have a nice evening." The Chauffeur said.

"You too," Heinrick said, then stepped out of the car and into the men's club.

The smokey room had two roaring fireplaces, a couch, wing chairs, and matching coffee tables. There were men playing chess or backgammon while talking, smoking their cigars, drinking their whiskey and or Bourbon. Two men stopped chatting and welcomed Heinrick to the fold.

"Welcome to our brotherhood." One of the older men said.

"Go straight ahead; one of your brothers is waiting for you." The other man said.

Heinrick thanked the men then left to introduce himself to the young man standing in front of the fireplace holding a glass of whiskey.

"Heinrick Müller," Heinrick introduced himself.

"Nice to meet you. Randolph Zigfield. People call me Randolph," Randolph responded.

The men shook hands.

Randolph's hair was blond and styled in a messy toss. His casual designer jeans and white linen sport coat screamed Rebellion.

"Is the whiskey here any good?" Heinrick asked Randolph.

"Not bad, for a stuffy place like this," Randolph said.

Randolph lifted his cocktail glass and swirled its contents. "Want one?" Randolph questioned.

"Sure." Heinrick answered then let Anna down.

"Herr öber," Randolph called the waiter.

The waiter came from holding a silver tray, and a white cotton napkin hung over his arm from across the room.

"Yes, Sir." The waiter responded.

"A cup of your best whiskey," Randolph said.

"We only have one kind of whiskey, sir." The waiter explained.

"Would you consider your whiskey the best?" Randolph asked.

"Yes," The waiter responded.

"Then get me your "best whiskey," Randolph jested.

"Yes, Sir." The waiter said and left the table.

"I'll take the bill," Randolph announced.

"Aren't all the drinks complimentary?" Heinrick questioned.

"Well, yes. That is why I can afford to buy you one." Randolph chuckled.

"A man with a sense of humor. I think we are going to be fast friends." Heinrick said.

"Are you related to Anna Zigfield?" Heinrick asked.

"I am. Anna is my favorite cousin." Randolph shared.

"How many cousins do you have?" Heinrick asked.

"Just one," Randolph said, then chuckled.

Heinrick laughed then said. "I am meeting Anna tomorrow to discuss a few things,"

"You will enjoy meeting her," Randolph responded.

"Let's grab those seats before anyone gets them," Heinrick said.

Heinrick took a seat by the fireplace and suggested Randolph take the chair in front of him. The waiter found Randolph and Heinrick, then served them their drinks.

"Enjoy." The waiter said, then left tend to the other guests.

"Do you know why they asked us to come?" Heinrick asked Randolph.

"My name is Lucas Wagner. It looks like we are the youngest here. Lucas said, adding himself to Randolph and Heinrick's mix.

"Welcome," Heinrick said.

"Anyone has an idea why we were summoned here?" Lucas asked.

"I was thinking the same question," Heinrick answered.

The lights flashed in the room, getting everyone's attention.

"Gentleman. Please step forward and take your assigned seats." Heinrick's father announced.

"We will find out soon," Randolph committed and walked ahead of Heinrick and Lucas.

When Heinrick united with Randolph and Lucas at the front row, he recognized his father as the night's main speaker.

"Dad?" Heinrick said surprised.

"Is that your father?" Randolph asked.

"Yes, it sure looks like him," Heinrick answered.

"Now things are getting interesting," Randolph concluded.

The chatter was silenced as the three young men took their seats.

"Let us get started by welcoming our three new members. Lucas, "please stand." Lucas will be responsible for Iran." Heinrick's father, Maximillian, announced.

All the men clapped for Lucas.

"Thank you, Lucas. Our next young man is Randolph Zigfield, cousin to the heiress, Anna Zigfield. Randolph, "please stand up." Randolph will be responsible for assisting Anna from Austria." Maximillian stated.

The men welcomed Randolph to the group.

Our third and final player is my son Heinrick. "Please stand up, Heinrick." You will be partnering with Anna Zigfield. Maximillian said.

The men applauded, welcoming Heinrick to the fold.

"Lucas, Randolph, and Heinrick, in this historic moment, you have been chosen to participate alongside Anna in her treasure hunt. You will each be given a sealed envelope with a clue written by King Johann Zigfield. He had a vision that included the three descendants of his three most trusted advisors. The numbers on the clues indicate the order to be followed. The clues are written for Anna to decipher and for you to assist. The clues are meant to lead Anna to an inheritance that has been kept secret until now. Men, if any of you do not want to continue in this venture, this is the time to speak up." Heinrick's father instructed.

"No problem here," Randolph spoke out.

"I am always ready for a challenge," Lucas said.

"If you give me my days off from the firm." Heinrick jested.

"Of course. Good luck." Maximillian nodded and excused the meeting.

Being curious about the clues, the three young men decided to open their envelopes before they left.

Heinrick was the first to read his clue that was labeled number one.

#1 *"Going back to the lion's den from whence you came."*

Lucas was the second to read his clue.

#2 *"If I am you, and you are me, which date would you be?"*

Randolph was the last to read his clue.

#3 *"If I watch, you will go. If you watch me, you will know."*

Anna's cousin Randolph replied, "I sure hope Anna knows more than we do about what we're doing." After that, they went their separate ways.

The following day, Heinrick arrived at the café early then asked to be seated at the table facing the entrance door. Before Heinrick took his seat, he draped his coat and scarf over the chair's back next to him then took his seat at the window.

"Are you ready to order?" The waiter asked Heinrick.

"Not yet. I am waiting for someone." Heinrick replied.

"Yes. Of course. No problem. I will be back later." The waiter responded then left.

When Anna entered the cafe, she recognized the description of Heinrick's coat and scarf. When Anna approached the table, Heinrick was reading the menu.

"Heinrick Müller?" Anna asked interrupting Heinrick.

"Yes, and you must be Anna Zigfield," Heinrick said.

"Yes, I am," Anna responded.

Heinrick stood up and helped Anna with her coat.

"Thank you," Anna said.

As customary, Heinrick kissed Anna's hand.

"It is a pleasure to meet you. "Allow me," Heinrick offered, then pulled the chair out for Anna.

As Anna took her seat, she quickly glanced at Heinrick and noticed his intelligent blue eyes.

"Forgive me for being forward; you look gorgeous," Heinrick said.

"Thank you," Anna responded shyly, thinking to herself, "That's a little bold."

Heinrick's imagination of Anna had not done her justice. Her long curly hair fell on her shoulders, framing her beautiful face, her jeans hugged her tiny waist, and the color of her sweater brought out her sparkling green eyes.

"Stop staring at her, and you are making her uncomfortable," Heinrick told himself.

Heinrick looked away and turned his attention to the menu.

Anna's mind wandered off as she noticed Heinrick's tall physic, those intelligent and expressive blue eyes, and dark hair cut fashionably.

"A cup of espresso, please, with an almond biscotti on the side," Heinrick told the waiter.

"That sounds good. I'll have the same." Anna agreed.

"Excellent choice. I will be back shortly." The waiter said, then left the room, leaving Heinrick and Anna to begin their conversation.

"How long have you been living in Vienna?" Anna asked.

"I was born and raised here," Heinrick answered.

"Same here except for the two years I spent in Iran before the revolution. We are very fortunate to have lived in such a beautiful city." Anna added.

In agreement, Heinrick gave Anna a warm smile and a nod.

"Besides being connected to the will, how did you get involved in my quest?" Anna asked.

"It was a condition handed down from the King to have one of the sons of the trusted advisors accompany you on your journey through each clue. Since my father became the executor of King Johann's will and I work with my father, it was decided I'd be the one to accompany you for the length of your journey to discover the treasure that awaits you." Heinrick explained.

"When does the treasure hunt start? How many players?" Anna asked as she sipped her espresso with a bite of her biscotti.

"The treasure hunt starts today. I have our first clue. There are four of us, including you." Heinrick explained.

"What's next?" Anna asked curiously.

My father has secured a private plane to take us where we need to go by the end of the week." Heinrick answered.

"And the clue?" Anna asked, raising her eyebrows.

Heinrick took out the clue from his pocket and handed it to Anna. Anna read the clue out loud.

"Going back to the lion's den from whence you came," Anna read.

Anna started thinking out loud, "The first thought that comes to mind is the story in the Bible of Daniel and the lion's den. Daniel had been thrown in the lion's den for not obeying King Nebuchadnezzar and choosing to worship God of Israel. A miracle had happened when Daniel had to confront what would have been vicious lions. Instead, Daniel was surrounded by docile lions. God saved his life that day." Anna said.

Anna then was stunned by the sudden realization that the Lord had done the same for her. God had saved Anna by softening Braham's heart for her instead of being held captive for 444 days as the rest of the hostages in the American embassy.

"Besides the lion in the story, I don't see the correlation," Heinrick remarked.

"When the time is right, I will explain. For now, I need you to trust me," Anna said.

"All right," Heinrick replied.

"The next clue is in Tehran at the former American embassy," Anna stated.

"As soon as we leave, I will make arrangements with my pilot to get us to Tehran by nightfall," Heinrick said.

"Is there anything else I can get you?" The waiter interrupted.

"Just the check, please," Heinrick said.

"Yes, sir." The waiter said.

The waiter took out the bill and lay it on the table.

"I have this covered," Heinrick said.

Heinrick paid the waiter then helped Anna with her coat.

Anna felt herself relax as she put her arms in the sleeves in her coat one at a time.

"You are such a gentleman," Anna said.

"Nothing but the best for you," Heinrick winked.

"You flatter me, Mr. Müller," Anna said as she batted her lashes.

"I am happy you feel that way," Heinrick said.

"I will need to take care of a few things, then meet you," Anna replied.

"I am glad you will be the one to accompany me. I feel like I can trust you," Anna said.

"I appreciate your faith in me," Heinrick said, grateful for Anna's sentiments.

"My driver will pick you up around noon. That gives us enough time to get there before dark." Heinrick continued.

"I will be ready," Anna smiled.

CHAPTER
Five

"For I, the LORD your God, hold your right hand;
it is I who say to you, "Fear not, I am the one who helps you."
Isaiah 41:13 ESV

The mid-afternoon canvas in the sky was graced with sapphire and pure milky whites. Anna looked out the plane's window and watched the cotton candy clouds.

Anna pulled down the window shade then leaned into her seat.

"Get some rest. We have a long night ahead of us. Would you like another pillow?" Heinrick asked.

"Yes, please," Anna answered.

Heinrick asked the flight attended for a pillow. "Could you please get another pillow for this lovely lady?"

"Thank you," Anna said.

"My pleasure," Heinrick responded.

"Here you go," The flight attendant commented, then handed Anna the small pillow.

Anna leaned back into her seat, adjusted her pillow, and closed her eyes. While Anna was dozing away, she saw Heinrick driving his car into a frozen lake as clearly as if she was there. Anna jolted out of her vision and opened her eyes in fear.

"It must have been a bad dream?" Heinrick said gently.

"It was," Anna responded.

"Want to talk about it? Heinrick asked.

Anna smiling at his kindness, shook her head no.

"Let me get you some water," Heinrick said.

That would be nice," Anna responded, grateful for Heinrick's thoughtfulness.

When Heinrick returned, Anna had covered herself with a blanket.

"You look cozy. Are you feeling better?" Heinrick asked, then handed Anna a glass of water.

"I do; thank you," Anna answered.

Six and a half hours later, Anna raised the window shade and looked outside. The plane started its descent by turning on its flight gear in the abyss of the starry night sky.

Heinrick fastened his seat belt then looked at Anna.

"Do you have your mandatory scarf to cover your head? Heinrick asked.

Anna took out her scarf from her bag, put it on her head, and tied it under her chin.

"How do I look?" Anna asked.

"Like you are wearing a babushka," Heinrick said, then chuckled.

"Really? "Anna played along.

"You would look beautiful with a bag on your head," Heinrick said.

"Hopefully, it does not come to that," Anna said, then chuckled.

"As soon as I get home, I'll ask Anna out on a date." Heinrick thought.

Gradually the runway came into sight. The city lights twinkled, the ribbon of cars turned life-size, the plane flashed its lights then tilted its wings in the runway direction.

"We are about to land," Anna said and fastened her seatbelt.

The plane dropped its wheels, flew closer to the runway until it landed on the pavement at full speed, and slowed down to a complete stop.

As soon as the pilot parked the plane, Heinrick and Anna were ready to step out of the aircraft.

"I'll call you when we are on our way back," Heinrick said.

"While waiting, get yourself something to eat," Heinrick offered, then took out one of his credit cards from his wallet and gave it to the pilot.

"Thank you," The pilot said.

Heinrick picked up the rental car and drove with Anna to what used to be the American Embassy. It was now covered in graffiti and painted with death to America messages. The former American Embassy had been turned into a museum of artifacts found by the hostage-takers. The current moniker for the former Embassy was The Den of Spies.

When Heinrick had reached his destination, he parked the car at the Embassy entrance.

"Oh, good. Lucas is here with the next clue," Heinrick told the pilot.

Heinrick got out of the car and walked around to open the door for Anna

"Lucas Wagner. Welcome to Tehran." Lucas greeted Anna enthusiastically as he walked towards her.

"Let's talk in my car. It's warmer in there. Lucas invited.

Anna and Heinrick agreed and followed Lucas to his car.

"What a beauty. What year?" Heinrick asked while looking at Lucas's Porsche.

"1979," Lucas answered.

"Great year for a Porsche," Heinrick said.

"All right, boys, less talking and more doing," Anna pronounced. Once in the car, Lucas gave Anna a clue.

"Here is your next clue," Lucas said, then handed Anna the envelope. Anna opened the envelope and read its content.

"If I am you and you are me, which date would I be?" Anna read.

After Anna had finished reading, she was distracted by another vision of a gated compound and a row of four faded house numbers.

Anna felt the necessity to share her vision.

"I had a vision," Anna replied.

"Ok," Lucas said, then took out a pencil and paper from his glove compartment.

"Can you draw your vision?" Lucas asked.

"I don't know. I haven't tried it," Anna said.

When the pen touched the paper, Anna's hand had a mind of its own. Anna's last vision had come to life once more.

"The faded house number must be the answer," Heinrick said.

"This might be far-fetched, but do you think the house number might be the same as the year and date the will was written?" Heinrich asked while looking at Anna's sketch.

"November 5, 1803," Anna said.

"Let us start deciphering the numbers," Lucas suggested.

"November is the eleventh month," Heinrich said.

"And the day is the fifth," Lucas replied.

"And the year is 1803," Anna responded.

"When we put the numbers in a row, we get 1151803," Heinrick answered.

"Could these set of numbers be both a house and coordinates?" Heinrick asked.

"Yes, I do," Anna said.

"Let's start with looking up a coordinate first," Lucas suggested.

Lucas took out a map from inside his glove compartment then lay it out on the dashboard. "May I look at the map?" Anna asked.

"Sure," Lucas said

"I found it." which brings us ... to here," Anna said, pointing to a considerable distance of wooded land on the map.

"I see it," Lucas said.

"It's a forest," Heinrick said in amazement.

"When I lived with my parents in Tehran, my dad and I hiked in that region. Now that I think of it, I remember seeing a house from a distance." Lucas said.

"I think you are on to something," Heinrick added

Lucas took out a second map and handed it to Anna.

Take my spare map; you might need it just in case we lose each other." Lucas explained then handed the map to Anna.

"Thank you," Anna responded

"Once we get close to the outskirts of the city, there will be no streetlights. We will have to depend on our high beams to see the road ahead." Lucas warned.

"Follow me after you turn your car around," Lucas continued.

"We will be right behind you the whole way," Heinrick said, then walked to his car with Anna.

"Ready?" Heinrick asked as he adjusted the side mirrors.

"As ready as I can be," Anna said and unfolded the map.

When Anna, Heinrick, and Lucas had gotten on the road, it had started snowing heavily.

"There he is," Anna said, pointing at Raham's car.

"I can hardly see anything," Heinrick responded.

The icy conditions slowed down the few drivers that were on the highway. Heinrick tried to keep up with Lucas and the weather by turning on the windshield wipers but to no avail. Within minutes, snow and ice had covered the entirety of the road. Heinrick leaned over the steering wheel and tried to see the road ahead.

"Can you see any signs?" Heinrick asked while squinting his eyes.

"There is a sign coming up on the right," Anna said.

Heinrick put his high beams and emergency blinkers on and slowly took the next turn off the highway and onto a dark and empty road.

"I think we're lost," Heinrick said.

Anna turned on the light switch over the rearview mirror and read the map.

"According to the map, we are heading in the right direction. However, we need to find a rest stop to wait for the snow to die down," Anna explained.

"There!" Heinrick exclaimed, referring to a rest stop.

Heinrick slowed down the car to take his turn when he noticed a road barrier.

Anna heard the Lord's gentle whisper in her ear.

"I am in control," The Lord whispered in Anna's thoughts.

"Keep breathing," Anna told herself.

"We are almost out of gas," Heinrick said.

"There might be a gas station off this road," Anna responded.

"I see a street sign!" Heinrick exclaimed, squinting.

"I see it too!" Anna confirmed.

While Heinrick tried to take his turn into the gas station, he lost control of the car's wheels. Heinrick clung to the steering wheel as hard as he could, his knuckles turned white, and his muscles rigid.

Heinrick had never been a religious man, but it did not stop him from reaching out to God.

"Please, God, stop the car." Heinrick cried out to the Lord.

"Could this be the moment my vision is being manifested? Anna reminded herself of the nightmare vision she had on the plane to Tehran.

Just then, the car slowed down then corrected itself.

"Did you see what I just did? That was amazing." Heinrick said and puffed up like a peacock.

Anna shook her head and rolled her eyes, thinking to herself that God may have had a hand in that save.

"Here we go," Heinrick assured and kept on driving.

Anna tried to follow the road by reading the map.

"According to the map, we only have an hour to go," Anna said.

After Heinrick got on the highway, the wind started bearing down on the small car, causing it to slide. The tiny vehicle fought back as if it were a bucking bronco, spun on its head like a Dreidel, turned around on its wheels, and stopped in the middle of the road.

"Are you hurt?" Heinrick asked, shaken yet confident

"I don't think so. What about you?" Anna asked while checking herself for any injuries.

"No more than rattled. I think I am getting the hang of driving in this weather." Heinrick said.

"Heinrick truly believes that in both instances, he was in control of the car," Anna thought in amazement.

"Once they were back on the road, Anna remembered they had needed gas for the car.

"How much gas is left in the tank?" Anna asked.

"Three-quarters of the way," Heinrick said.

"I thought you said we were running out of gas?" Anna asked, amazed.

"I must have read it wrong," Heinrick answered.

"Lord, I see you," Anna prayed to herself.

"Could you please check the map and see if we are still driving in the right direction," Heinrick asked.

"Looks like it," Anna answered, looking up from the map.

While Heinrick and Anna were at the mercy of the dark and narrow road, Anna had another vision. It was dark like the road they were on until light broke through the darkness, and a tender voice said.

"Behold, the Devil will be testing you." The voice warned Anna in her thoughts.

As far as the eyes could see, trees were dressed in shimmering white gowns, and the moon was like a phantom-silver halo surrounded by dazzling stars. In time, Anna remarkably closed the gap between Johann and herself among the stars and the moon in the night sky.

"Can you see the spotlights moving in the sky? They seem to be coming from the top of that mountain." Heinrick replied, interrupting Anna's vision.

"Watch out!" Anna screamed.

The van swerved on the icy mountain, colliding with Heinrick's car, and threw him off the mountain's edge. The automobile flew into the frozen lake and knocked Heinrick unconscious. Anna's head jolted, and her seat belt tightened around her chest, making it hard for her to breathe. Islands of ice encircled the car like sharks preparing to devour their prey. The automobile shook as it landed on the riverbed; The water broke through the windows with the force of a broken fire hydrant. Anna fought against the rising waters and felt her seat belt crushing her chest one last time. It was not until Anna saw Heinrick 's body float past her that she took her last breath.

"Swim towards the light." the Angel of God told Anna.

Suddenly, Anna opened her eyes and tried to see past the murky waters.

"God has not finished writing your story." The angel said, appearing to Anna.

The angel used the tip of his wing to clear the murky waters, revealing the fullness of his glorious wings. Then he scooped Anna and loved her in the warmth of his soft feathers.

"There." The angel replied, reassuring Anna.

The angel showed Anna the way out, opened his wings, and gently nudged her as if she were a chick gently pushed to fly for the first time.

"I found her!" The soldier yelled.

"Grab the rope." another soldier called out to Anna.

Anna held the suspended rope while lifted out of ice-bound waters. She was given a blanket covering her body and hair. Then she was escorted to the white van and put into the back seat.

Anna hunched down in the van, shivering under the blanket. She did not notice Heinrick sitting next to her.

"Hi, beautiful," Heinrick said.

Anna turned around, stunned to see Heinrick sitting next to her.

"I thought you were dead," Anna uttered while holding back her tears.

"I assure you I'm very much alive," Heinrick said, shivering. Anna was shivering, too. Heinrick calmly reached for one of Anna's hands and put it on his chest.

She felt a sense of calm as he took her hand. She could feel Heinrick's steady heartbeat as well as his firm and muscular chest under her hand and the sensation of fluttering butterflies in her stomach while she silently thanked God; they were both alive.

"I cannot imagine life without you." Heinrick said tenderly.

"Of course not. I am the best thing that ever happened to you." Anna joked and sat up, grinning from cheek to cheek.

"Even when she almost died, she can lighten the mood." Heinrick thought, admiring Anna's courage.

"Yes. One of a kind." Heinrick nodded.

"Now that's the spirit," Anna said, then chuckled.

Anna stopped talking when she heard the soldiers getting closer to the van.

"The soldiers are coming," Anna whispered.

The soldiers jumped into the van and drove up a mountain towards the spotlights Heinrick had seen.

"Something feels wrong," Anna whispered.

"I feel it too," Heinrick agreed.

"What do we do?" Anna asked.

"We wait," Heinrick answered.

Anna watched the road ahead and looked for anything that she could recognize from her visions. The gate matched the same gate in her vision, along with the house number. As the van drew closer to the entrance, Anna noticed Lucas sneaking inside the compound as she watched him jump into the back of a moving van.

"Lucas is in the compound," Anna whispered.

"Where did you see him?" Heinrick spoke softly.

"I saw him jump and hide in one of those trucks," Anna whispered.

Heinrick looked for Lucas among the many vans parked in the driveway.

The van stopped at the gate and waited to be let in by the surveillance guard. Once inside, the soldier parked the vehicle in front of an old mansion.

Meanwhile, Cyrus was sick of seeing Braham's version of himself reflected in his mirror. He had considered covering all the mirrors in the house, but that would have made him seem unfit to be a leader.

Even with Cyrus's efforts to hide his true identity, he knew he lived on borrowed time.

"It was not supposed to be this way," Cyrus said while adjusting his silk tie.

Shahid knocked at Cyrus's door.

"Come in," Cyrus said.

"The soldiers rescued a man and a woman from a car accident at the lake, Dariush has them waiting for you in the sitting room, and the Lieutenant is waiting to see you. Shahin said.

"Have the lieutenant meet me in the office. I will deal with our new guests later." Cyrus ordered.

Cyrus had his back to the door and admiring the painting on the wall when the Lieutenant entered the room.

"Van Gogh, I bought that from an auction not too long ago when I was promoted to chief of this operation," Cyrus said.

"It's a beautiful piece; I love how the colors blend, expressing the true nature of the artist." The Lieutenant said.

Cyrus turned to the Lieutenant and asked him to sit.

"Come sit," Cyrus invited and pointed the Lieutenant to the chair in front of his desk.

Cyrus stepped into the sun and obstructed the flow of light.

"What can I help you with?" Cyrus asked.

"I have a job for you." The Lieutenant said, then placed a picture of his wife on the desk.

Cyrus reached into his desk drawer and took out a contract.

"Do you have anything else besides this picture for me?" Cyrus asked.

The Lieutenant took out a folder from his briefcase and handed it to Cyrus. Cyrus looked through the papers then slip the contract to the lieutenant.

"Sign here stating you agree for me to take care of your problem and below this line that you will be paying me two thousand rials to get the job done," Cyrus said.

"Do it fast. Even if my wife was unfaithful, I still love her." The lieutenant said.

"You need not worry. It will be short and sweet just like this." Cyrus said, then took out his gun from under his desk and shot and killed the Lieutenant.

"Soldier," Cyrus called out.

"Yes? sir." The soldier said while entering the room.

"Clean this mess up," Cyrus ordered.

"Yes, sir." The soldier said and dragged the lieutenant's body out of the room.

In the interim, a revolutionary flag and a portrait of Ayatollah Khomeini greeted Anna and Heinrick when they entered the building.

"Give him your coats," Shahin said while walking ahead.

"Come in. Let me get you something," Dariush said.

Shahin immediately recognized Anna and decided to make her Cyrus's problem. He sneered as he walked away.

When Anna recognized Shahin, she felt the room closing in on her, her stomach churn and an overwhelming desire to flee. Heinrick felt Anna's anxiety and discreetly held her hand. When Heinrick locked fingers with Anna, she experienced a peace that overshadowed her fears.

Anna and Heinrick reluctantly handed their coats and were accompanied by Dariush to the seating room.

"Can I offer you some hot tea?" Dariush asked.

"No, thank you," Heinrick responded, keeping his eyes on Anna.

Anna noticed a commotion behind Dariush. Dariush was speaking while a large black body-sized bag rolled down the stairs and landed behind Dariush. Dariush looked behind him, shook his head, and cringed at sight.

"Pick it up." The soldier holding the bag said.

"Don't get touchy; I am trying." The soldier on the other side said. "A lot is going on here," Anna whispered, trembling slightly.

"You don't know half the story," Dariush mumbled, then left the room and closed the door behind him.

"You two. Get this out of here before Cyrus notices," Dariush warned the soldiers.

Heinrick decided to speak to Anna as soon as they were alone.

"What happened with you in the foyer? I saw your face go white when you saw the two men that met us at the door." Heinrick questioned.

"Do you remember the American hostage take over in 1979 in Iran?" Anna asked.

"Yes," Heinrick answered.

"Well, I was temporarily one of them. The rebels in the embassy took hostage anyone working at the American Embassy. So, I helped a friend get her father out. Her father was a chef there. And in the process, I was captured.

"That's a lot to take in." Heinrick acknowledged.

"It was," Anna agreed.

"No wonder you reacted the way you did. How long did they keep you?" Heinrick asked.

"Now that's when things got interesting. The ringleader helped me escape a few hours later." Anna answered.

"That is interesting. I wonder why?" Heinrick asked.

"Maybe he saw something in me that reminded him of someone he cared for," Anna answered.

"I'm also confident that prayers had something to do with my escape. I saw a longing in Braham's eyes." Anna continued.

"I suppose that makes sense," Heinrick said apprehensively.

"The worst part is these guys move in packs," Anna responded.

"They sound like wolves," Heinrick surmised.

"They are." Anna agreed.

Anna thought of the cruel irony of her circumstances.

Anna looked out the arched windows, wondering what happened to Lucas. At that moment, Lucas appeared in the window with his eyes wide open at seeing Anna staring at him. Heinrick saw what Anna was looking at and rushed to the window to let Lucas inside.

"Hey. You guys were not going to leave me behind, were you?" Lucas asked while climbing through the window.

You can't leave yet. I have another clue." Lucas said.

"We are not going anywhere without you," Anna promised.

"What is this place? What happened to you guys?" Lucas asked, concerned. He noticed that Anna and Heinrick were still both wearing their wet attire.

Anna updated Lucas with events from getting lost to their near-death experience.

"I can't imagine what you both had to go through, but I can tell you it was not in vain," Lucas said. Lucas reached into his right pocket and took out a key which he then handed to Anna.

Anna took the ornate miniature key and began investigating it.

"Where did you find this?" Anna asked.

"I came to this house following the coordinates we deciphered and found the key behind the house number. I waited for you two to show up. When you didn't come, I backtracked and saw a couple of soldiers putting you in a van." Lucas explained.

Inspecting the key, Anna said, "Looks like two turtle doves sitting on a branch."

"And a partridge in a pear tree?" Heinrick sang.

Anna handed Heinrick the key. "Yeah, No partridge," Anna said, clearing her throat with a smile.

Anna appreciated Heinrick's joking. It was just what she needed to help get her mind off Shahin and Dariush, whom she anticipated seeing on the other side of the door.

"Two doves and a branch? Hmmm." Heinrick said, then gave Anna the key back.

Anna took the key then made an announcement.

"For now, this is where it's going to go for safekeeping," Anna said, then put the key in her bra.

"I wonder what the key belongs to?" Lucas asked.

"Must be somewhere on this property," Heinrick guessed.

"Let's go. Anna insisted.

Before leaving, Dariush walked into the room with dry clothing, demanding that they change before presenting them to Cyrus. Lucas had quickly hidden behind the window coverings. Anna and Heinrick quickly changed behind some screens in the room. In a few minutes, they were ready to go.

"Cyrus, our chief lieutenant, is ready to see you," Dariush said.

Dariush took a double-take and saw shoes poking out from under the curtains and a partially opened window.

"I do not remember letting you in the house?" Dariush called out to Lucas.

Lucas sheepishly came out from behind his hiding place.

"I will let Cyrus deal with you," Dariush said.

After Dariush had spoken to Cyrus, he motioned the three to follow him.

"Follow me to Cyrus's office," Dariush said.

"Your hair is showing," Heinrick whispered.

"Thank you," Anna said, then repositioned the scarf Dariush had given her.

As they walked into Cyrus's office, the atmosphere changed dramatically. Where Dariush had been accommodating, the climate in the room was now tense and threatening. All three, Anna, Heinrick, and Lucas, felt the change. Dariush walked over to Cyrus and whispered in his ear. As Cyrus listened, his eyes narrowed, and he laughed.

When Anna saw Cyrus, she was perplexed.

She thought, *"This is Braham, isn't it?"*

Braham had once taken favor to her; would he do it again? But Anna noticed this man's eyes were different from her previous captor. Braham, the man she had prayed for, had sad, melancholy eyes, while the man who was glaring at her was dark and frightening.

"My name is Chief commander Cyrus. You two, take a seat. Cyrus ordered, nodding toward the two chairs in front of his desk.

"Not you." Cyrus harshly said to Lucas.

Cyrus called Shahin and gave orders to lock Lucas in the basement. Lucas, ready to protest, looked at Heinrick, who warned him to stay quiet with a barely noticeable shake of his head.

Cyrus looked at Anna with a sardonic grin, which sent chills up her spine.

"I didn't get for your name," Cyrus questioned Anna.

"You know her name," Braham said, echoing in Cyrus's mind

"Your name?" Cyrus asked Anna again.

"Anna," Anna responded.

"Your WHOLE name," Cyrus said, agitated.

"Anna Zigfield," Anna answered. Her thoughts reflected on the words, *"The devil will be testing you."*

Anna's fear turned to anger at the thought of Satan's victory over Braham. Then, with a solid conviction to continue praying for him, a sense of tranquility came over her.

Cyrus watched the fear drain from Anna's countenance and be replaced with calm confidence. He became furious as he felt his authority challenged.

"Let her go. She and her friends are no threat to you." Braham insisted.

"She is not yours to keep," Braham said.

"Excuse me, sir, but we have an engagement elsewhere," Anna said politely.

Shahin, who had reentered the room, was ordered to take Anna to the harem.

When Shahin led Anna outside the room, Anna tried to break away by stomping hard on Shahin's foot. "Ouch! Whore! Not this time!" Shahin said, then grabbed Anna's arm and took her to the harem.

Once Shahin and Anna reached the harem, Shahin pushed Anna into the Eunech's arms.

"She is all yours! Shahin shouted at the Eunuch.

"This time, no one is letting you go." Shahin sneered to Anna, then stormed out of the room.

"As for you," Cyrus told Heinrick.

"Let them go!" Braham said, causing Cyrus to feel a tinge of pain.

Cyrus stopped in mid-sentence, called his soldiers into the room for a drastic effect, and ordered his men to lock Heinrick in the basement.

"Put an end to this," Braham yelled.

"Make sure he can't escape. If he does, it's on you." Cyrus demanded.

"Yes, sir." One of the soldiers said.

Before Heinrick had exited the room, Cyrus had to have the last word by mocking Heinrick.

"It was a pleasure meeting you," He said sarcastically.

Cyrus watched his soldiers from his window, stacking weapons in the van, then checked the time, ensuring they were not running late.

"Get going. These guns are not going to sell themselves!" Cyrus yelled from the window.

"You don't need the money from this shipment." Braham insisted.

Cyrus planned to use his soldiers as bait to catch the men who had been stealing his merchandise. For him, his men were as valuable as the job.

"You care," Braham said.

"What I care about is the money," Cyrus said agitatedly.

"There is another way," Braham said, inching closer to his conscious.

"I am an assassin. There is no other way." Cyrus said while grinding his teeth.

Immediately pain like a sharp knife pierced through his eye, causing him to feel dizzy.

"You are not real. You are a symptom of my migraine!" Cyrus yelled at Braham.

Then he took Aspirin and went to bed, hoping his migraine would go away.

While Cyrus was sleeping, Braham woke up, put on his robe and slippers then headed directly to Dariush's bedroom.

"Dariush? Are you awake?" Braham asked, then knocked at the door.

"Dariush got out of his bed and opened his door to see whom he had thought would be Cyrus standing outside.

"Is everything okay?" Dariush asked nervously.

"It is me, Braham," Braham said gently.

"Why is Cyrus playing mind games with me? How do I respond without making him mad?" Dariush asked himself.

"Ester was your first love," Braham continued.

"I only told Braham about Ester," Dariush thought.

"My brother!" Dariush exclaimed.

Dariush and Braham hugged like the two best friends they were.

"It's been too long, my brother," Braham said.

"How long have you been subjecting yourself to Cyrus's dictatorship?" Braham asked.

"Since the day you transformed into Cyrus," Dariush answered.

"Why stay? When you could have left." Braham asked.

"Because you are my best friend, and I was not going to give up on you," Dariush answered.

"I cannot thank you enough, but I can handle things on my own now. It is time for you to live your own life," Braham insisted.

"No one, thing, nor circumstance in your life can separate you from me." Braham heard the Lord's comforting words whisper in his heart.

"However, before you leave, I do need you to free Anna and the two men that came with her. Most importantly, my beloved friend, leave this place and don't look back." Braham replied.

"How can I be convinced that you will survive, Cyrus?" Dariush asked.

"I have been able to catch glimpses in Cyrus's mind recently. So, it's just a matter of time before I get rid of this parasite in my mind." Braham answered.

Affectionately, Dariush touched Braham's shoulder and squeezed it slightly.

"Go! before Cyprus wakes up." Braham urged.

When Braham was slipping back into bed, Dariush was getting closer to the Haram.

Once Dariush had reached the Haram, he carefully walked into the room where the concubines were peacefully sleeping. The smell of sweet Jasmine was still in the air. After the women had finished grooming each other, they had bathed in the shared pool with Jasmine oil. Dariush felt a breeze and realized the sheer curtain door to the courtyard was slightly open; he cautiously opened the doorway and saw Anna sitting by the pond's edge. The canopy of stars and a full moon lit the skies as Dariush drew closer to Anna.

Anna looked up when she caught sight of a shadow and heard footsteps approaching her.

"Don't be afraid," Dariush said while coming into Anna's view.

"What do you want from me?" Anna asked defensively.

"I am not here to hurt you; on the contrary, I am here to help you escape," Dariush said.

"Why?" Anna asked apprehensively.

"It's about time I did the right thing, plus I am keeping my word to my dearest friend," Dariush explained.

"You can trust him." Anna heard the angel say.

"Your friends will be joining you soon," Dariush promised.

"Okay," Anna spoke softly, then nodded.

As Dariush climbed down the stairs, he realized that he had never been in the basement before. He wondered why until he took his last step into the underground chamber. The sizeable hollow space smelled like mildew and sweat. Dariush found the switch on the wall and lit the room surrounded by metal cages and a square table at the corner with a neat line of torture tools. Above the table hung keys to open the cells.

"Cyrus has lost his mind," Dariush thought,

Dariush picked up the keys from the wall and started his search for Heinrick and Lucas.

When Dariush had found the two men, they were sitting in their cages with their heads down.

Dariush then unlocked their cages.

"Ahead is your way out. Once you are out of the basement, keep going straight. You will reach a fork in the road where you will take your first right. Continue the path, and you will reach the back entrance of the courtyard. Anna will be waiting for you there," Dariush instructed. Then let Heinrick and Lucas out.

"Thank you. You are a good man," Lucas told Dariush.

"What are you waiting for? I have a date with a beautiful woman!" Heinrick said excitedly.

When Dariush walked into the covered courtyard, Anna was sitting at a pond's edge and mesmerized by the water flowing through her fingers and the goldfish swimming under the pink water lilies.

When Anna saw Dariush, she stood up.

"Listen carefully. When your friends get here, unlock the door by the evergreen bush. It will take you into a room where you will have access to an exit door." Dariush instructed, then handed Anna a key.

"Once you get into the secret courtyard, you will be safe. Not even Cyrus knows about its existence," Dariush assured, then left Anna alone with her thoughts.

"Thank you, Lord, for being a faithful and merciful God." Anna prayed.

After Anna had prayed, a small sparrow flew by Anna. Anna instinctively put out her hand and waited for the bird to land on her palm. But, instead, the chubby sparrow flew past Anna's open hand, hopped on her lap, looked up at her, and chirped gleefully.

"Hi, little guy," Anna said.

The sparrow chirped again then flew into a nearby tree.

"Hi, beautiful," Heinrick said, startling Anna.

Astounded, Anna looked up to see Heinrick smiling down at her.

"Your timing is always perfect," Anna heard herself say, then stood up.

"I try," Heinrick winked, then embraced Anna.

"This way," Anna urged after hugging Heinrick back.

CHAPTER
Six

"I will say of the Lord,
"He is my refuge and my fortress,
My God in whom I trust."
Psalms 91:2 NIV

With the arrival of Heinrick and Lucas, Anna took the key Dariush had given her to unlock the door to safety. They entered a room where towering arches with windows hung over each door. An artist used mosaic tiles to create vibrant birds with green, red, and blue feathers flying midair on the arched entranceways and door. Finally, the artist had finished his masterpiece by painting a meaningful story of a concubine's life on the walls.

"May I see the key Lucas gave you?" Heinrick asked Anna.

Anna took the key out of her bra and handed it to Heinrick.

"Sorry, it's warm," Anna smiled.

"As long as it is not sweaty, I am fine." Heinrick chuckled.

"You two are too funny," Lucas said.

"After completing the treasure hunt, we should take our show on the road." Heinrick chuckled.

"Works for me!" Anna laughed.

"And now, ladies and gentlemen, Heinrick and Anna will be entertaining you by playing in this treasure hunt," Lucas announced, then laughed at himself.

Anna and Heinrick looked at each other, then joined Lucas in humor and broke the tension in the room.

"It would make sense if the two turtle doves are hiding amongst these birds," Anna said.

"Where would we start looking?" Lucas asked.

"We can each take a door," Anna answered.

Anna searched for the doves by starting from the bottom of the arch then moving into the center.

"I found it," Heinrick said.

"That was fast," Anna replied, surprised at the short time it had taken him to find the keyhole.

"Where was it?" Lucas asked.

"Right by the handle. Between the two doves," Heinrick said.

Heinrick tried to insert the key in the keyhole, but it did not fit.

"Let me try," Anna said and tried to do the same but ended up with a similar result.

"Let me make an effort," Lucas said and aligned the key to the handle.

"It won't turn," Lucas said, disappointed.

"Back to the drawing board," Heinrick said.

"Another American saying you picked up?" Anna asked Heinrick jokingly.

"You guessed it," Heinrick said with a tender smile.

Anna felt Heinrick tugging at her heart then refocused on her situation at hand.

"I'll take the door closest to me. You guys choose from the other three." Anna instructed.

The room once admired became an overwhelming ménage of birds for Lucas and Heinrick to decipher through.

Lucas and Heinrick left Anna to start their search.

Anna sat on the floor cross-legged and tried to remember what her father would have told her if he was in her situation.

"All things are possible through Jesus Christ," Anna recalled.

"All right, then, where are you hiding?" Anna asked the doves.

Anna looked up and recognized the sparrow watching her with his head tilted on one side and perched on the glass ceiling.

"I remember you," Anna told the bird.

"You know where the key is, little guy. Don't you?" Anna asked.

"Hey! Guys! Help me look!" Anna called out.

Heinrick and Lucas joined Anna's search until she found a tiny mosaic drawing of two doves huddled together while sitting on a tree branch at the bottom corner of the door.

"May I have the key again?" Anna asked Lucas. Lucas gave Anna the key and watched.

Anna inserted the key in the keyhole and turned it clockwise. The lock made a clicking noise releasing the first cylinder.

"Now what?" Lucas asked.

"Patience..." Anna answered.

Anna turned the key anticlockwise and felt a second cylinder unlock the door. When Anna pushed the old door, it creaked and groaned like a cranky old man. Spiders had used their web to weave a doily that covered the entrance to the underground tunnel. Anna pulled aside the spider web and proceeded into the cold and damp passageway.

"We are right behind you," Heinrick said.

On each side of the tunnel, a fire torch supplied with its matches hung on the walls. Heinrick and Lucas each lifted a torch and lit it while waiting for Anna to do the same.

When Anna lifted her torch, a piece of paper fell from behind it.

"I found the clue," Anna said, then picked up the paper from the ground.

"What does it say?" Lucas asked.

"You can find what is old and turn it into new it all depends on you." Anna read.

"*What can be old and new at the same time?*" Lucas wondered.

"*Who is the "you"?*" Lucas pondered.

"Anna," Heinrick said confidently.

"How can I change the old to new?" Anna asked.

"Put on your archeologist hat," Heinrick answered.

"Old:" pertains to the old way of communicating by using Hieroglyphics, and "turning:" Translating and "new:" is the language of the present, Anna explained.

"Therefore, we are looking for Hieroglyphics on one of these walls," Heinrick concluded.

It had taken hours of walking, getting lost, and Anna's sprained ankle to find the symbols on the wall.

"Looks like this is it," Lucas said.

"This is amazing. I have seen Egyptian Hieroglyphics in history books but never in person." Anna said.

Anna evaluated the symbols facing her, and it became more apparent to her that God was stretching her faith by challenging her to use all the gifts he had given her.

Anna took her time remembering what she had learned from her textbooks.

"That looks like *Hear,* and this one seems to communicate the word *roar* and that one?" Anna questioned herself momentarily.

Anna ran her fingers on the jagged stone.

"The next is water. Yup, that's it!" Anna said confidently.

This looks like a *bath*. Hmmm, maybe that one symbolizes the *moon*?" Anna questioned.

"And the last one?" Lucas asked.

"Got that one. That says the *star.*" Anna answered.

"All right then, we have the words *Hear, Roar, Wall, Bath*, and *Star,*" Heinrick repeated.

"Hear the roar?" Lucas asked.

"Hear the roar. Bath goes with water," Heinrick added.

"Hear the roar of the wall of water," Anna finished.

"You took the words right out of my mouth," Heinrick responded.

"Bathing under the moonlight star," Lucas proclaimed proudly.

"Hear the roar of the wall under the moonlight star," Anna said excitedly.

"It's a waterfall," Lucas announced.

"Let's find that waterfall," Heinrick declared.

The morning sun broke through an opening in the ceiling of the shimmering cave, and a bright rainbow arched over the waterfall. The waters cascaded over the rocky ledge and loudly splashed into a pool below.

"God's handiwork is truly magnificent." Anna thought to herself.

"You look like you are in much pain," Heinrick told Anna.

"I'll be okay. I just need to rest my ankle for a little while." Anna responded.

"I am carrying you," Heinrick decided for Anna.

Heinrick swooped Anna over his shoulder and kept on walking.

"I am not a bag of potatoes," Anna complained in jest.

"And I am not carrying you over the threshold," Heinrick said light-heartedly.

"Maybe you will someday." Anna thought to herself.

When Heinrick and Anna caught up with Lucas, he had already been in the cave and standing at the water basin.

"The basin is precisely aligned to the open ceiling," Lucas said.

"Does that look right to you guys?" Lucas asked, referring to the pinhole in the ceiling.

"The positioning of the hole is placed directly over the basin," Heinrick answered then let Anna down.

"Bathing under the moon night sky," now it makes sense," Anna said.

"It's strange to me that the clue ends here," Heinrick added.

"Unless... the basin is the place to take a bath under the stars," Anna guessed.

"And the home to our next clue," Heinrick surmised.

Anna's thoughts wandered to a place where the stars and moon were reflecting off the basin's waters, causing its mouth to open wide and reveal a box under the bottom of its lip. Before Anna snapped out of her vision, she saw a second box.

"Did you have a premonition?" Lucas asked.

"Yes," Anna answered.

"And?" Heinrick prodded.

"We are looking for two treasure boxes, not one. One of the two boxes is inside the lip of this basin," Anna said then hobbled to the basin and sat by its side.

Anna checked the integrity of the basin before she put her hand in the water.

"Anything?" Lucas asked.

"Don't rush her," Heinrick urged.

"I am feeling an indentation in the lower lip and what feels like a small stainless steel box." Anna described.

"That must be the box we are looking for," Lucas replied.

Anna wrapped her fingers around the small box and tried to lift it, but it would not budge.

"I almost... had it," Anna said, disappointed.

"Let me try." Heinrick offered.

"Please be careful," Anna pleaded and stepped out of Heinrick's way.

The water was clear enough for Heinrick to see the bottom of the basin.

"This could easily become a death trap," Heinrick concluded.

"How is that?" Anna asked.

"Come here. Let me show you what I am talking about." Heinrick answered.

"See these large electronic coils? The slightest touch will trigger these coils and create a tornado effect. Let me put it to you this way. Once the coils in this basin are triggered, water will spin like a washing machine on steroids. Hence a tornado effect." Heinrick explained.

"Like being in a blender," Lucas added.

"I get it, guys. I do, but I have to try again." Anna insisted.

"She is right. We have come too far for us not to finish what we have already started." Lucas agreed.

Anna repositioned her body, making it possible to dislodge the box from under the basin's lip.

"I have it," Anna said.

Anna gripped the handle, released the small box, which floated to the top and bounced on the water. While Anna was reaching out for the container, her hairpin landed at the bottom of the basin, activating the coils. Heavy currents pulled Anna into the furious waters, flung her in the air, and dropped her at the bottom. The ravine bottomed out in response to Anna's weight, causing Anna and the box to roll out onto the ground.

Anna woke up to the frozen snow biting her wet skin and stray pinecones rubbing her flesh. Anna shivered uncontrollably and remained on the ground, looking up to see the sun dancing between the towering Evergreen trees. The height of the trees bought shame to the tallest building, and the rich aroma of Evergreen trees brought memories of celebrating Christmas with her family. A familiar sparrow flew by Anna, holding a worm in his beak. Anna remembered the three incidences that a sparrow had come to her when she had needed the Lord.

"Is this God's way of speaking to me? Anna wondered.

"Anna!" Heinrick and Lucas's voices echoed in the vastness of the woods.

Anna carefully pushed herself up while making sure she had not broken any bones. Besides a few scratches and a mild headache, Anna had survived the odds again. Joy filled Anna's heart as she understood God's role in her survival.

"Anna!" Heinrick yelled.

"I am here!" Anna cried out.

Lucas stopped and listened.

"I hear her," Lucas said.

"Anna! keep calling!" Heinrick yelled back.

Heinrick and Lucas followed Anna's voice until they found her sitting underneath a large tree.

"Are you injured?" Heinrick asked anxiously.

" Besides a mild headache, I am fine," Anna answered.

"How could she have survived from drowning and, even more amazing, she is not injured?" Heinrick thought, dumbfounded.

"You have to stop doing this," Heinrick said kiddingly, holding Anna close to him.

"Are you warm enough?" Heinrick asked.

"Yes. Sorry, life keeps getting in the way," Anna responded with a smile while looking up at Heinrick.

Heinrick tucked his hand under Anna's lower back, lifted her, and carried her in his arms.

"Is that better?" Heinrick whispered in Anna's ear.

"Yes," Anna said quietly.

Anna, Lucas, and Heinrick saw lights from a small house located deep inside the forest.

"Maybe the homeowner in that house will be kind enough to let us call the pilot," Heinrick said. Then helped Anna stand.

"Seems to be our best chance to get home," Anna concluded.

"Let's keep going," Lucas encouraged.

Heinrick rang the doorbell and waited for someone to answer the door.

When Dariush opened the door, he was as bewildered as Anna and her friends to see them standing in front of him.

"What happened?" Dariush asked Anna.

"It's a long story. Can we come in?" Anna asked.

Dariush noticed Anna favoring her left ankle.

"Please come in and rest your foot. Of course, gentlemen, come in, come in," Dariush invited.

"Please take a seat. Can I get all of you tea and some sweets?" Dariush asked.

"That sounds so good. Yes, please," Anna answered.

Heinrick and Lucas simultaneously nodded their heads in agreement.

"Dariush, thank you for all you have done for us. How can we thank you?" Heinrick asked.

"Someday, when I come to your house, you can serve me your tea and sweets," Dariush answered with a big smile.

"That sounds like a perfect plan," Anna said.

"May I use your phone?" Heinrick asked.

"Of course. My house is your house." Dariush answered, then left to the kitchen.

Heinrick had made the necessary arrangements for him and his friends to depart when Dariush returned from the kitchen.

Dariush walked into the room with a platter of desserts, sugar cubes, and four tea glasses. After putting the platter down, he dispersed the tea, handed out dessert plates, put a sugar cube in his mouth, and washed it down with hot tea.

"Don't be shy. Take as much as you want," Dariush offered.

Anna and Lucas filled their plates with Almond cookies, Halva and Baklava.

"This is delicious," Heinrick said.

Anna nodded her head in agreement with a mouthful of Halva and forgetting momentary that Dariush had been one of her hostage-takers in Tehran.

"You are not whom I thought you were," Anna told Dariush.

"I had fallen with the wrong crowd. It's incredible what a person would do to be accepted. I will always regret being a part of taking the American's hostage. I still have nightmares of those wretched days," Dariush said.

"You are not the same man. Your past should not define you," Anna said.

Dariush could hardly believe what he was hearing.

"You are very kind," Dariush said, looking into Anna's eyes

"Everyone deserves a second chance," Anna said, then smiled at Dariush

"I have a serious question for you," Anna said.

"Okay," Dariush said, afraid of what Anna would ask.

"What is this incredibly delicious dessert made of?" Anna asked and put another piece of Halva on her plate.

"Sesame paste, pistachios, and sugar," Dariush chuckled.

"Everything is scrumptious," Lucas said, then put a sugar cube in his mouth and washed it down with his tea.

"Do you live here?" Lucas asked.

"Yes. I like it here." Dariush answered.

"Don't you worry, Cyrus will find you?" Anna asked, concerned.

"No. My house is the safest place for me to be," Dariush answered.

"How is that?" Anna questioned.

Cyrus is afraid of coming to this side of the forest. It has something to do with his childhood." Dariush explained.

"What about his soldiers?" Anna asked.

" Anyone who is associated with him has to do the same," Dariush explained.

"He is a disturbed man," Anna said sadly.

"Not for long," Dariush replied.

"May I drive all of you to your destination?" Dariush asked.

"That would be much appreciated," Anna answered.

CHAPTER
Seven

"I will deliver you out of the hand of the wicked
and redeem you from the grasp of the ruthless."
Jeremiah 15:21 ESV

As soon as Anna came home, she immediately took the box with the jewelry to the bank and personally placed them in the bank's main vault, then went home to call her mother.

After the first ring, Tanya picked up the phone.

"Hi, sweetie, I just got off the phone with Heinrick, who told me everything. I am so sorry you went through all that. Is there anything I can do to help?" Tanya asked.

"You can give me a hug," Anna answered.

"Of course, I will. I had the chef make you your favorite meal, Schnitzel, with a side of potato salad." Tanya said.

"That sounds amazing!" Anna exclaimed.

"In all honesty, how is my baby girl doing today?" Tanya asked, referring to Anna.

"If it were not for the grace of God, I would not be here," Anna answered.

"I wholeheartedly agree. You had an Angel watching over you the whole time," Tanya said.

"Yes, I did. I'll see you soon," Anna responded.

"Can't wait. I love you." Tanya responded.

"I love you more," Anna said, then hung up the phone.

Anna was lured to the kitchen by the irresistible fragrance of Schnitzels frying on the stove. When Anna walked into the kitchen, she saw Randolph sneak a piece of cake and eat it. Anna and Randolph were cousins who had grown up together and, as kids, had become inseparable.

"Hey. That's tonight's dessert. Hand me a piece too." Anna teased.

"Cousin, you are home! Randolph said excitedly. Then walked up to Anna and hugged her with his sticky hands.

"Oh no! You didn't!" Anna said, pretending to be upset. Then rubbed her piece of cake in Randolph's face.

"Now you're in trouble!" Randolph teased, then wiped the cake off his face.

Randolph grabbed another piece of cake and held his hand up.

"Don't do it," Anna warned.

Randolph grinned like a Cheshire cat then ate the slice of cake. "This is yummy," Randolph said.

"I missed you while you were gone," Anna replied.

"Back at 'cha. Bring on the shenanigans." Randolph announced.

"He goes to America for six months and comes home sounding like, What 'cha?" Anna said.

"A handsome cowboy," Randolph finished.

"Okay. I'll give you that." Anna said.

"So much has changed since you were away. Did my mother tell you what she learned from my friend Heinrick?" Anna asked.

"Is Heinrick your boy... friend...?" Randolph teased. "

"You are so juvenile," Anna said.

"Anna and Heinrick sitting on a tree. K. I. S. S. I. N. G," Randolph sang.

"Is that all you got from Heinrick's story? That I might have a boyfriend?" Anna asked.

"Yup," Randolph answered.

"I have the next clue," Randolph said.

"Are you talking about the treasure hunt?" Anna asked. "

"Yes," Randolph answered.

Randolph searched his pocket then took out an envelope.

"Hold on to that till tomorrow," Anna requested.

"All right. How about we go fill our tummies with a whole lot of yummies?" Randolph asked.

"You're such a goof," Anna responded.

"Yeah, but you love me anyway," Randolph said.

"I sure do." Anna voiced.

Randolph made kissy noises then ran towards the dining room.

Anna playfully ran past Randolph while sending him back his kisses.

"Hey, me first. No fair!" Randolph yelled after Anna.

"Life isn't fair. Anna said, giggling, then ran down the hall. Without watching where she was going, Anna ran into Heinrick standing at the front door. Heinrick pretended to keel over with pain.

"I am so sorry. Are you okay?" Anna asked, feeling mortified.

"Couldn't be better," Heinrick said, laughing and beaming at Anna.

"Randolph brings the kid out of me," Anna explained, hoping to deflect from her embarrassment.

"By the way, I invited Heinrick for dinner!" Tanya called out from the dining room. "

"I can see that," Anna said while looking up and smiling at Heinrick.

"I am glad she did," Heinrick whispered.

"She cleans up nicely," Randolph told Heinrick when passing him to the dining room.

"She gets more beautiful each time I see her," Heinrick agreed.

Once everyone had entered the dining room, the Butler made his announcement, " Dinner is served."

When Anna and Heinrick took their seats next to each other, they secretly locked their fingers together.

Heinrick squeezed Anna's hand affectionately, causing her stomach to flutter.

"Though it seems we are very formal here, we are not," Randolph announced.

Randolph took off his shoes and put them next to his chair.

"There you go," Randolph said.

"Randolph, must you?" Anna said, slightly annoyed.

"Yes. He must." Tanya chuckled.

"Everybody, take off your shoes and relax," Tanya played along.

Anna shrugged her shoulders then broke into laughter.

"No food fights until next time," Randolph promised.

The entire table broke into laughter, and the Butler chuckled while serving the food.

Before leaving, Anna hugged her mother and kissed her on the cheek.

"Thanks for tonight. You always know what I need." Anna told her mother.

"Thank you for making me feel part of your family," Heinrick said earnestly.

"You're both welcome," Tanya replied.

"I will see two of you at nine am sharp tomorrow," Randolph told Heinrick and Anna.

"I forgot to mention. I will be spending the rest of the week with your Tanté Maria. She is feeling very lonely and has been having a hard time dealing with your father's death." Tanya said.

"Tanté Maria is my dad's sister," Anna told Heinrick.

"Family comes first," Heinrick replied.

"Good luck with your treasure hunt, and please be careful," Tanya urged.

CHAPTER
Eight

"I will deliver you out of the hand of the wicked
and redeem you from the grasp of the ruthless."
Jeremiah 15:21 ESV

During the eclipse in Braham and Cyrus 's minds, Cyrus watched Braham's film of memories.

Cyrus was infuriated after he had learned about Dariush's betrayal. Ravished with a vengeance, Cyrus grabbed his robe, put on his slippers, and commanded to see his soldiers.

"Find Dariush. Find the prisoners. Find them all. No one, I mean NO ONE! betrays me and gets away with it!" Cyrus yelled.

"Yes, sir!" The group of soldiers said in unison then hurried to their vans.

After Cyrus's soldiers had left the premises, Cyrus made a phone call to one of his Federal Government contacts.

"Her name is Anna Zigfield. Get me everything you can find on her." Cyrus said.

Cyrus checked in at the Ritz-Carlton in Vienna, told the clerk that he did not want to be disturbed, paid the bellboy for bringing up his luggage, and locked the door behind him.

Cyrus dialed the number to the front desk.

"Yes. How can I help you?" The clerk asked.

"Where do I sign up for a tour of the city?" Cyrus asked.

"I can help you with that. There is a city tour starting tomorrow from 9:00 am. Would you like me to sign you up? The clerk asked.

"That would be fine. Thank you for your help." Cyrus answered.

"You are welcome, sir." The clerk said, then hung up the phone.

Cyrus had planned every detail of his trip to Austria. He would pack enough clothes for a week's stay, find Anna, eliminate her, then finally spend the rest of his week sightseeing in Vienna.

When Cyrus got himself settled, he went to the main lobby to speak to the concierge.

"I need a ride to Stadtpark," Cyrus told the Concierge.

"Yes, sir." The Concierge said.

Then made a call to arrange a Limousine to pick Cyrus up at the hotel.

The car stopped at the Ritz-Carlton and waited for Cyrus.

The bellman opened the back door for Cyrus to enter.

"19th district Döbling," The bellman told the driver.

The driver nodded his head then drove away,

"We have nice weather today. I hope you are enjoying our city?" The driver asked.

"Oh. Yes! I have been looking forward to this day." Cyrus said enthusiastically, then checked his watch, ensuring that everything was going to plan.

"Are we ready to finish this game?" Randolph asked Heinrick and Anna.

"Yes." Anna and Heinrick answered in unison.

"Love your eagerness," Randolph said, then handed Anna her next clue.

Anna took the sealed envelope, opened it, and read the clue out loud.

"If I watch you, you will go. If you watch me, you will know." Anna read.

"Who is watching you?" Heinrick asked.

"Okay. So that's creepy." Randolph said.

A vision interrupted Anna's thoughts. King Johann, in his portrait, turned his head and looked straight at Anna.

"We don't even know what this guy looks like," Randolph said.

Randolph's voice brought Anna back to reality.

"I do," Anna said, then left Heinrick and Randolph to the library.

"I remember seeing an oil painting in the library," Randolph shared.

When Anna, Heinrick, and Randolph entered the library, Randolph was first to notice King

Johann's portrait was hanging over the fireplace.

"That is King Johann of Engelman," Anna replied while feeling a solid connection to the painting.

"It's all in the eyes," Anna said.

"You are right," Heinrick said, following Johann's eyes to the writing desk in the room.

"If I watch, you will go. If you watch me, you will know." Randolph repeated the clue.

Heinrick aligned himself to King Johann's eyes in the painting and followed it to the writing desk in the room.

When Heinrick got to the desk, an envelope addressed to Anna Zigfield lay in the middle of the table.

He picked up the envelope sitting in the center of the writing table and handed it to Anna.

"Nicely done," Anna told Heinrick, then ripped the envelope and removed the card.

"Well? What does it say?" Randolph asked.

"Ringing and singing come together in one meaning," Anna read.

"Somewhere among these books has to be the answer to our next clue," Randolph said.

"We have ringing and singing that are supposed to add up to one meaning?" Anna questioned.

"I'll look for a book titled "Ringing and singing," Randolph suggested.

"I'll help you look," Heinrick offered.

"I'll take a different approach; I'll figure it out as I go," Anna said.

Anna's looked through many books before she had found the right one. Anna's instincts drew her to a book titled *"Songs of the heart."* Johann Zigfield authored the poetry book. Anna turned the first page and read: *"To my soul mate. You make my heart sing."* Signed: *Johann*

Anna searched the pages until she discovered a bell inside a cutout between two pages.

"I found something!" Anna exclaimed.

Heinrick and Randolph stopped what they were doing and turned to Anna.

"I found the ringing to the singing," Anna said.

"You found what to a what?" Randolph asked.

"Let me show you," Anna answered.

Anna took out the bell and looked underneath it. "The next clue," Anna responded. Then removed the paper from inside the bell.

"That's impressive," Randolph said.

Anna unfolded the note and read the clue out loud.

"Push me, and you will see the home of my wife and me." Anna read.

Anna put the poetry book back from where she had found it and held onto the clue.

"What if the Rebels found out where King Johann lived and tracked him to this villa?" Heinrick asked.

"In the time Johann built this house, many of these villas had secret rooms, Randolph explained.

"What I hear you are saying is we are looking for a hidden room," Anna concluded.

"I wonder if the poetry book is not done helping me decipher the clue?" Anna pondered.

Instead of taking the poetry book off the shelf, Anna pushed the reader further in creating a domino effect. The antique shelf made a click sound then slid open, revealing a curved staircase.

"Perfectly done, cous," Randolph told Anna.

Anna smiled then nod her head in the direction of the stairs.

Heinrick, Anna, and Randolph climbed down the stairs to what seemed to be the king's hidden quarters.

"Can you handle spider webs?" Randolph asked daringly.

"I don't know. Can you?" Anna asked.

"There is a spider on your head!" Heinrick yelled.

Randolph screamed and spun himself around while trying to get the spider out of his hair.

Yes, He is." Heinrick and Anna said, then they burst into laughter.

"Hilarious guys," Randolph responded, trying to keep himself from laughing.

A kitchen, living room, and two small bedrooms made Johann and his family a cozy home.

"Let's conquer and divide. I'll start with the first bedroom, and you boys can begin by looking in the kitchen," Anna said.

When Anna entered the narrow bedroom, she saw a family painting of King Johann, Queen Antoinette, and their young prince and princess. Anna's heart sank with sadness as she envisioned the Royal family without a kingdom to rule. Heinrick stood behind Anna and wrapped his hands around her waist.

"You would have been a beautiful princess," Heinrick told Anna.

Anna picked up a framed photo from the bedside table.

"This looks like King Johann and queen Antoinette on their wedding day," Anna said.

"I did not see it until now. There is an uncanny resemblance between you and Queen Antoinette," Heinrick replied.

"Anna and Heinrick. I could use your help here!" Randolph called out from the kitchen.

"On my way." Anna and Heinrick said in unison, then left the room.

There were wide open empty cabinets, dishes in and around the sink, silverware, and pots and pans on the countertops.

"Has there been a robbery?" Anna joked.

"There is no room to swing a cat in here," Randolph said while trying to keep a straight face.

Laughter filled the room again.

Anna stood on her toes to search the cabinets. When she got to the last cabinet, she felt an envelope wedged in the corner. Anna pulled the envelope out of the cabinet and dust it off, then read its content.

"When I slumber, I think of Lumber," Anna read.

"Slumber meaning Sleep," Heinrick said.

"Sleep in your bed," Anna finished the thought.

"Lumber, the bed, is made out of lumber," Randolph added.

" So is the floor underneath the bed," Heinrick chimed in.

"The jewelry box is in the bedroom under the bed," Heinrick concluded.

"It has to be under one of the planks," Anna added.

"I am on it," Randolph said, then rushed into the bedroom.

"I am coming too," Heinrick said while following Randolph.

" I'll clean up this mess alone," Anna said, speaking to the empty room.

"Give me a hand with the bed," Randolph asked Heinrick.

Heinrick squeezed himself to the side of the bed.

"Is it me, or is this bed too big for this room?" Heinrick asked.

"According to their photograph, it's a good thing neither of them was overweight," Randolph chuckled.

Randolph pulled the mattress off the bed and leaned it against the door.

"Ready at the count of three?" Heinrick asked.

"Yes," Randolph answered.

"1...2...3," Heinrick counted.

At the count of three, Heinrick and Randolph lifted the bed and set it against the wall. Then sought a weak spot on the floor by tapping their feet on the individual slats.

Meanwhile, Anna was organizing the kitchen cabinets when she felt an evil presence.

All along, Cyrus had been lurking in the shadows waiting for the right time to kill Anna.

"Well, well, well... look who I finally found," Cyrus said, standing behind Anna.

Anna turned around and saw Cyrus staring down at her.

Anna felt like a trapped animal; every fiber in her body screamed for help, yet her voice had betrayed her.

"*Think!*" Anna pleaded to herself.

Anna carefully picked up an iron-clad pan behind her, hit Cyrus with it, and watched him fall. Empowered by her newfound bravery, Anna found her voice again.

"Heinrick!" Anna screamed and ran towards the bedroom.

Before Heinrick could hear Anna, Cyrus had gotten up and caught up with Anna.

Prior to Anna screaming again, Cyrus came from behind her and covered her mouth.

"You. Stupid girl," Cyrus whispered in Anna's ear.

Cyrus's moist breath against Anna's neck made her nauseous. If only she could break away from him, she would hurt him again.

"It's me, little mouse," Braham said, and gently released her.

"Braham?" Anna said, astonished that she had recognized Braham.

"Yes. Forgive me for all Cyrus made you go through." Braham responded.

"There is nothing to forgive; you were not yourself," Anna said knowingly.

Braham felt himself slip away.

"Run!" Braham yelled abruptly.

But it was too late. Cyrus grabbed Anna by her throat and started to choke her. Braham felt the heat of Cyrus's rage rushing through his veins, helping him to overpower Cyrus. Braham broke Cyrus's grip but not before Cyrus stabbed Anna in her chest.

" I am so sorry," Braham wept while holding Anna.

"Go. They won't understand," Anna said weakly.

"Thank you," Braham said, then left the scene.

When Heinrick and Randolph heard the screams coming from the kitchen, they pushed the bedframe out of their way and ran to Anna, who was covered in blood.

"Anna. what happened." Heinrick panicked, then helped Anna on the couch.

Randolph put the jewelry box down on the coffee table then sat on Anna's other side

"May I?" Randolph asked.

"Yes," Anna replied.

Randolph lifted Anna's shirt to exam her stab wound.

"You need to go to the hospital," Randolph concluded.

"Wait, not until you promise me that both Jewelry boxes are safely in the bank," Anna pleaded.

"I promise," Randolph said.

CHAPTER
Nine

"Be still and know that I am God."
Psalms 46:10 NIV

As soon as Anna arrived at the hospital, the doctors rushed her to surgery.

"How bad is it?" Randolph asked one of Anna's surgeons.

"I will know better after the surgery." The surgeon answered.

"What would you do if you were in my shoes?" Heinrick prodded.

"Pray." The surgeon suggested.

"As soon as I have any news, one of the nurses or I will let you know." The surgeon said compassionately and left to tend to Anna.

"She'll be fine. You'll see," Randolph promised Heinrick.

"I'll be in the chapel," Heinrick said.

The quaint chapel held its own in the enormity of the hospital. It had seen many people from different walks of life enter its doors and leave with a new sense of hope. Heinrick took his seat at the front pew and sat in silence until he felt a sense of belonging and turned his attention to the cross on the altar.

"God, if you exist, please don't let Anna die." Heinrick pleaded.

Since his parent's separation, Anna was the only person who had given Heinrick hope that he was not doomed to make the same mistakes his parents did. Anna made Heinrick feel like he mattered. "Are you there, God?" Heinrick asked the Lord.

"The Lord hears you." The angel of God answered gently.

The angel's voice consoled Heinrick like the warmth of a dawn blanket on a cold winter's night.

"Trust the Lord. He cherishes you, and His love calls out to you." The angel said.

Heinrick heard a singing sparrow.

"He will never leave nor forsake you." The angel promised.

The sparrow flew and landed close to Heinrick.

"How did you get in?" Heinrick asked the little bird.

"Nothing is impossible with God." The angel said.

Heinrick 's thoughts betrayed him by taking him to the source of his guilt.

The night Heinrick was eighteen and had one drink too many, and his buddies had offered to drive him home.

"If only... I had not been trying to impress my friends. I would not have crashed into that car and almost killed two people. If only..." Heinrick pondered.

Before the angel continued to speak, the sparrow hopped on Heinrick's lap and let him stroke his tiny head.

"What if God could take away all your guilt? What if all you have to do was believe in God's forgiveness?" The angel asked.

"Why would I do that? I don't know him." Heinrick said.

"Because God never stopped loving you. Let me tell you your story until now. God was the one who protected the couple you hit and saved you from going to prison. God took the wheel while you were driving on the icy roads in Tehran, and it was God who saved you from drowning a short while after," The angel said.

Heinrick could not deny God's miracles anymore and burst into tears.

"Can you see God's love for you?" The angel asked tenderly.

"Yes," Heinrick responded in the stillness of his heart.

"Heinrick. Come!" Randolph said, running into the chapel.

"Is Anna okay?" Heinrick asked nervously

"Better than okay. See for yourself." Randolph said.

"I'll stand out here making sure no one interrupts you and Anna," Randolph said.

"Thank you," Heinrick replied.

"I gotcha back." Randolph told Heinrick.

"Don't mind him. He thinks he is so "cool," Anna called out.

"Like a handsome cowboy," Randolph added.

Randolph, Anna, and Heinrick broke into laughter.

"Go get her," Randolph told Heinrick, then pat him on his back.

When Heinrick entered the room, Anna gave Heinrick a warm smile.

Heinrick was amazed at how well Anna looked.

Heinrick sat on the bed and held Anna's hand.

"I missed you," Anna said.

"I never left," Heinrick said, then gave Anna an affectionate smile.

"I got used to your never-ending presence and annoyance." Anna teased.

"I'll have to make up for that," Heinrick chuckled.

"I am counting on it," Anna smiled.

"May I kiss you?" Heinrick asked gently.

"I thought you would never ask," Anna said.

Heinrick drew closer to Anna and tenderly kissed her on the lips. Anna returned the kiss and looked into Heinrick's eyes.

"I love you," Anna said tenderly.

"And I love you," Heinrick said, then kissed Anna's lips once more.

Heinrick sat by Anna's pillow and hugged her gingerly. Anna permitted herself to become vulnerable. She released all her pain and opened a floodgate of what felt like endless tears.

"I am sorry." Anna whimpered.

"For what?" Heinrick asked.

"For dragging you in this mess," Anna said.

"I would do it all over again for you," Heinrick responded.

Heinrick wiped Anna's tears and held her face in his hands.

"It's over," Heinrick said softly, then moved closer to Anna's pillow.

"It's not over yet. I had a premonition while I was sleeping. Cyrus was suffocating me with a pillow." Anna whispered.

"I have an idea on how to bring all this to an end. Do you trust me?" Heinrick asked.

"With all my heart," Anna answered.

"I will need you to do something for me," Heinrick replied.

"All right," Anna said.

"Play along," Heinrick replied.

Anna nodded her head yes.

"Randolph, you can come in now," Heinrick called out.

"It's about time. I was growing roots while waiting in one spot," Randolph chuckled.

"Thank you," Anna told Randolph.

"You are welcome, cous," Randolph said.

"It will be over soon," Heinrick whispered, then kissed Anna on the nose.

"Do you guys need more time to be alone?" Randolph joked.

"We are fine," Heinrick chuckled, then left the room to call his friend, the Detective.

"Hi princess," Tanya said, surprising Anna.

"Mama!" Anna exclaimed with open arms.

"I am sorry it took so long to get here," Tanya responded, then carefully hugged Anna.

"All that matters is you are here now," Anna replied.

"Mrs. Zigfield, it is so lovely to see you. Heinrick said while entering the room.

"Call me Tanya. You are practically family." Tanya replied.

"Tanya, it is," Heinrick agreed.

"Anna, I am going to speak to your surgeon and will be back soon," Heinrick hinted, then left to see the detective.

"What does he need to ask the doctor?" Tanya asked.

"Never mind him. He worries." Anna answered.

The detective and Heinrick had agreed that the best way to catch Cyrus would be for the detective to go undercover as one of Anna's surgeons.

"My name is doctor Hoffanburg. I was one of your previous surgeons. How are you feeling?" The Detective asked.

"Hurting," Anna answered.

While the Detective was speaking, the real surgeon walked in.

"I don't think I have seen you before." The surgeon told the Detective.

"I am new to this hospital." The Detective said.

"Welcome." The surgeon replied.

"Thank you." The Detective responded.

"What is your pain level from one to ten?" The surgeon asked Anna.

"Seven," Anna answered.

"Would you mind writing out the prescription?" The surgeon asked the detective.

"No problem, I can do that," The detective replied.

"You lost much blood, Anna. It is a miracle that the knife didn't puncture your heart." The surgeon continued.

"Another miracle," Heinrick thought, thanking God for this time.

"When can I go home?" Anna asked eagerly.

"You should be able to go home in a few days with bed rest for at least ten days," The surgeon answered.

"I will make sure of that," Tanya said.

"So, will I." Heinrick chimed in.

"Count me in," Randolph added.

"Good," The surgeon said, then left the room.

The Detective waited for the surgeon to go back to his rounds before he asked everyone in the room to leave.

"Would you mind leaving the room while I do a quick examine?" The Detective asked.

"Not at all," Tanya said.

When the Detective was alone with Anna, he took the opportunity to share what he and Heinrick were scheming.

"Follow my lead," The Detective said.

Heinrick and Randolph followed Tanya into Anna's room.

"The nurse will be in to administer your pain medication. That should help you sleep," The Detective told Anna.

"You rest, my love. We will be here when you wake up." Tanya said.

"I am feeling tired," Anna replied.

"I'll be in the visitors' lounge," Heinrick told Anna.

"I know a café close by that has the best coffee and pastries," Randolph said.

"Sounds good," Tanya responded.

"Have a good snooze," Randolph said.

Heinrick watched Tanya and Randolph take the elevator then went back to sit with Anna.

After Cyrus had stabbed Anna, he prevented Braham from leaving the Villa, allowing him to hear Heinrick telling Randolph the hospital he would be taking Anna.

"*That was easy. So very easy,*" Cyrus had told himself, then stole Anna's car and drove to the hospital.

Cyrus took the elevator and got off on the surgery unit. He walked the halls until he saw a doctor standing at the nurses' station. When Cyrus approached the Detective, he was pretending to be studying a patient's chart.

"Could you please direct me to Anna Zigfield's room?" Cyrus asked the Detective.

"And your name?" The Detective questioned.

"Heinrick," Cyrus lied.

"One Moment." The Detective said, then picked up the phone and dialed Anna's room. Heinrick answered the phone.

"Heinrick is here to visit you." The Detective said.

Heinrick hung up the phone and eagerly waited for Cyrus to walk into the room.

"He is here. Isn't he?" Anna asked anxiously.

Heinrick nod his head yes, then hid behind the door waiting for Cyrus.

"Follow me." The Detective said.

The closer Cyrus got to see Anna, the more excited he became.

"This is Anna's room," The Detective mentioned.

"I can taste the victory." Cyrus thought.

"Thank you," Cyrus replied, then entered the room.

"Welcome to Austria," Heinrick said sarcastically and put Cyrus in a stronghold.

Cyrus kicked Heinrick in the shin and broke free.

"Not so fast." The Detective said, walking into the room and pointing his gun at Cyrus. Cyrus attempted to get his gun from his pocket.

"One more move, and I will shoot." The Detective warned.

Cyrus quickly grabbed his gun, and the Detective shot him.

Braham prevented Cyrus from hitting his head on the edge of the bed by victoriously reclaiming his mind, then started slipping onto the ground.

"Help him," Anna urged Heinrick.

Heinrick helped Braham lean against the wall next to Anna's bed.

Anna carefully got out of bed while holding onto her I.V stand, then cautiously sat on the floor and put Braham's head on her lap.

"Why are you helping me?" Braham asked weakly.

"It's my turn to stay by your side," Anna said.

When Braham felt himself slip away, he had expected to be carried away to hell. But the peace that followed was none he had ever felt. Joy filled Braham's soul as he watched his mother and sisters standing next to Jesus, who was waiting for him with open arms.

"You are finally free," Anna promised.

"Follow me to the kingdom of God." the angel of God said.

Braham felt his soul separate from his earthly body.

"You are home," The angel told Braham and lit the path to heaven.

CHAPTER
Ten

**"Rejoice in the Lord always.
I will say it again: Rejoice!"
Philippians 4:4 N.I.V**

Heinrick decided to drive to the Austrian Alps a day earlier and ask Tanya and Randolph for Anna's hand in marriage three weeks later. The scenic drive was what Heinrick had needed to calm his nerves before he arrived at Zigfield's chalet.

Three Weeks Later

Tanya saw Heinrick drive up the circular driveway and ran to meet him at the door. "I am thrilled that you are here a day earlier," Tanya replied, then entered the house with Heinrick. Randolph heard Heinrick's voice and met him in the foyer.

"Welcome, old chum," Randolph said.

"Did you travel to Britain recently?" Heinrick chuckled.

"Are you asking because of my new and approved British accent?" Randolph asked, then chuckled. "Yes," Heinrick answered.

"That's all I got in British English. Y'all wanna follow me to the back patio?" Randolph asked.

"I reckon I do," Heinrick played along.

"Good for you; you are catching on," Randolph winked.

"How does fresh lemonade sound to you boys?" Tanya asked while entering the patio.

"Sounds wonderful," Heinrick answered.

The lake's waves crashed against the rocks, and the bright orange sun suspended over the waters.

"It's beautiful here," Heinrick replied.

"It is my most favorite place on earth," Randolph said.

"I can see that." Heinrick agreed.

Tanya Joined Heinrick and Randolph at the back porch, then handed out the cups of lemonade.

"What a perfect day," Tanya said. Then took a sip of her lemonade and closed her eyes, breathing in the fresh air.

"How are you doing?" Tanya asked Heinrick.

"Never better," Heinrick answered.

"Please, Lord, let them say yes." Heinrick prayed to himself.

"As you must know by now, I am deeply in love with your daughter. Therefore, I would like your blessing to ask her to marry me," Heinrick said.

"We would be overjoyed. Right? Randolph," Tanya asked.

"Welcome to the family," Randolph announced, then hugged Heinrick tightly while lifting him off the ground.

"Put him down. He is going to think we are crazy and change his mind to marry Anna." Tanya told Randolph.

"It is too late for that," Heinrick said.

Randolph put Heinrick down, and laughter filled the air.

A week later, Heinrick planned a seamless night to propose to Anna. The doorbell tinkled when Heinrick entered the Floral Shop. "Good morning. How are you doing on this fine day?" The Florist asked.

"It is a beautiful Spring Day," Heinrick answered.

"You are very chipper today," The florist stated.

"Are you looking for something special for your someone special?" The Florist questioned.

Yes." Heinrick answered enthusiastically.

"Is this the special day?" The Florist's wife asked.

"Yes, it is," Heinrick replied.

"How do you know about his special day?" The florist questioned his wife.

"While you are busy hearing yourself talk, I was listening to our customers," The Florist's wife said.

"This is what you can look forward to," The florist joked.

"Don't listen to him." The Florist's wife responded.

"Come here." The Florist teased his wife, then squeezed her cheeks and kissed them.

"Stop it!" The Florist's wife giggled.

The florist kissed his wife again.

"We can continue this later," The florist flirted with his wife.

"You wish, old man," The Florist's wife chuckled.

"Let's not scare the boy from proposing," The Florist said, then gave his full attention to Heinrick. "Unless Anna says no, nothing is going to stop me from marrying Anna," Heinrick said.

"That's how it should be," The Florist said.

"You are in luck. A new shipment of Red and White roses arrived earlier this morning." The florist's wife replied.

"Make sure you choose our best roses!" The Florist told his wife, then smiled at Heinrick. She gathered all the Red and White roses and brought them to the front for Heinrick to see.

"They are beautiful. Anna will love these," Heinrick said excitedly.

"How many would you like in your bouquet?" The Florist's wife asked.

"I will take them all," Heinrick answered.

The Florist started counting the roses on the counter.

"We have four dozen roses," The Florist surmised.

"I hope your sweetheart is not allergic to Roses," The Florist laughed.

"Don't jink it. Old man," The Florist's wife added.

Heinrick laughed.

After the Florist had finished the last bouquet, Heinrick paid the Florist and headed out to the door. "Congratulations!" The Florist and his wife said in unison.

"She will have to say yes first," Heinrick said.

"I am sure she will!" The Florist exclaimed.

"Thank you. Have a wonderful day," Heinrick said, then left the store.

When Heinrick got to Anna's apartment, he prepared breakfast for Anna and himself.

"This is delicious. You are full of surprises, Mr. Müller." Anna said, taking her first bite.

"How about I surprise you some more?" Heinrick replied.

Heinrick opened the refrigerator door and took out a picnic basket.

"We are going on a picnic at the park," Heinrick said.

"I am liking the way this day is going so far," Anna responded.

It was a perfect day in the park. Four little ducklings were paddling their little feet in the water while keeping up with their mother when a duck dove into the pond, splashing water in their faces. The smell of spring blossoms and dog owners playing with their dogs made for the ideal backdrop for Heinrick's next surprise.

"Come with me. I have a surprise for you." Heinrick invited.

"Another surprise?" Anna asked.

"I am just getting started," Heinrick replied, then took Anna's hand and led her to the dog adoption booth.

"We are adopting a dog!" Anna said excitedly.

"Not just any dog," Heinrick said, then showed Anna the white Schnauzer looking up at her.

"I love him," Anna said, reaching out to the miniature Schnauzer.

"Would you like to pick him up?" The volunteer asked.

"Yes, please," Anna said.

"Why would anyone want to give you up?" Anna asked the Schnauzer.

"His previous owner had to move and couldn't keep him anymore." The volunteer said.

The schnauzer licked Anna's face and tugged at her heart.

"Someone is in love." The volunteer smiled.

"Looks like it's mutual," Heinrick agreed.

The dog snuggled into Anna's arms.

"It would be against all that is good in this life to separate these two," Heinrick said.

"Would you want to go home with me?" Anna asked the dog.

"He comes with his leash and collar." The volunteer mentioned.

The dog barked at Anna and wagged its tail.

"Sounds like a yes to me," Heinrick said.

Anna and Heinrick filled out the proper paperwork.

Then Anna and Heinrick left the dog adoption booth and found a shaded spot to sit.

"Did you know about this little guy before you brought me here?" Anna asked.

"Yes. The Moment I saw the Schnauzer, I thought of you." Heinrick answered.

"When I was in college, my white Schnauzer had died. I never got over that." Anna shared.

"I know your mother told me," Heinrick said.

Anna's eyes swelled up with tears.

"You are the kindest and most thoughtful man I have ever known," Anna said, then kissed Heinrick with deep affection.

"He is perfect. Aren't you, my little man? You look like a Max." Anna told the dog.

"I am feeling like the third wheel." Heinrick pretended.

"You are my man too," Anna told Heinrick, then leaned into him.

"Keep that thought. You will need it for my next surprise." Heinrick teased.

"This day keeps getting better," Anna thought.

Anna and Heinrick spent the rest of the day enjoying Max.

"Time goes by fast when you are having fun," Heinrick said.

"Is it too soon to say it feels like Max, you, and I are a family?" Anna asked shyly.

"I was thinking the same thing," Heinrick answered.

When Anna and Heinrick were at the car, Heinrick stopped Anna from opening the car door. "Remember I told you I had another surprise for you?" Heinrick asked.

"Yes," Anna said.

"Close your eyes," Heinrick said.

Heinrick blindfolded Anna's eyes.

"Just making sure you don't peek," Heinrick said.

Heinrick walked Anna and Max down a private path and into a secret garden where Tanya, Rupert, and Katie waited.

"Here we are," Heinrick said, then took off the blindfold.

Anna opened her eyes to a candlelit path that led to shimmering lights in and around a gazebo. A table dressed in linen with red and white roses and lit votive candles in crystal containers sat under a crystal chandelier. Sheer curtains danced to the wind's soft melody, and the perfume of Roses filled the night air.

"It's stunning. Heinrick," Anna replied.

Heinrick kissed Anna's hand then pulled the chair out for her. After Heinrick took his seat, he was taken back by Anna's beauty.

"You take my breath away," Heinrick said. Heinrick took the ring box out of his pocket, pushed his chair back, went down on one knee in front of Anna, and opened the ring box.

"In these few weeks, you have shown me what it means to have a family and feel whole again. You have blessed my life with your kind and unconditional love. Your faith has led me to a life I could have never imagined for myself. When I am with you, God reminds me how deep his love is for me. Anna Maryann Zigfield, will you be my wife?" Heinrick asked.

"Yes. Thousand times, yes!" Anna said, then stood up and wrapped her arms around Heinrick. Max barked.

"Okay, buddy. We love you too." Heinrick said.

Anna picked Max up and held him in her arms, then kissed his little head.

"I love you," Anna told Heinrick, then kissed him on his lips.

"I love you," Heinrick responded, then returned Anna's kiss tenderly.

"Save some of that for your honeymoon," Randolph said while entering the Gazebo with Tanya.

"Welcome to the family," Tanya told Heinrick with arms open. Heinrick walked into Tanya's embrace.

"Now come here, let me give you a hug," Randolph said.

"That's okay. I'll pass." Heinrick chuckled.

"This is a day I will cherish for the rest of my life," Anna replied.

"I know; my being here took it over the top." Randolph chuckled.

After a year of planning, the big day had finally come.

"You look stunning," Tanya told Anna.

"Yes, you do." Katie agreed.

"When are you going to tie the knot?" Tanya questioned.

"Who me?" Katie asked, playing innocent.

"You are the only bachelorette in this room," Anna said.

"I have seen the way you and Randolph look at each other.

"Hmmm..." Tanya added.

"Those longing Bambi's eyes say it all," Anna teased.

"Today is your day," Katie said while keeping her and Randolph's secret.

"Nice way to change the subject," Anna remarked.

"I am so happy for you," Katie replied, then gave Anna a long hug.

"Stop, my makeup. You are going to make me cry," Anna responded.

"I am going downstairs to check on the guests. I'll see you soon." Katie said, then left the room.

The designer had used tulle, delicate lace, and satin to create the wedding dress that flawlessly defined Anna's petite figure. Anna stood in front of the standing mirror and modeled her dress. "Your father would have been proud of his little girl," Tanya remarked while watching Anna in the mirror. "I have your something blue," Tanya added.

Anna turned around to see her mother taking out a monogrammed blue linen Handkerchief. Anna took the Handkerchief and noticed the monogram.

"Antoinette," Anna replied, astonished.

"This handkerchief has been handed down to every woman in the Zigfield family on their wedding day. One day you will hand it down to your daughter. Your father left it for me to pass on to you on your wedding day. He would have been so happy to be here with us."Tanya said.

"Thank you, Mama," Anna replied, holding back her tears.

"Here is something new," Tanya said and handed Tanya plane tickets.

Anna looked at the tickets and jumped with joy, then hugged Tanya.

"Be careful with your hair," Tanya laughed.

"There is enough hairspray in my hair to cement it to my head," Anna said and broke into laughter. "Paris, London, Spain, and Greece!" Anna said while bursting with joy.

"Your father and I took the same Honeymoon," Tanya remembered.

"It must have been a great experience, Anna replied.

"Not until we went back the second time," Tanya winked.

"Why?" Anna asked.

"We were too busy experiencing ourselves," Tanya answered.

"Scandalous!" Anna responded, then laughed.

"And your something old, Tanya said.

Tanya took out a piece of Royal jewelry one piece at a time.

"Let me help you," Tanya offered and closed the latch on the necklace.

"Thank you," Anna said, admiring each piece of jewelry.

"Now you are ready," Tanya replied.

Heinrick waited for Anna next to an arch decorated with red and white roses under an old weeping willow tree. As soon as the violist started playing the Waltz, Heinrick watched his gorgeous bride walking towards him in awe.

Anna walked down the aisle of wildflowers towards her handsome groom. Her heart danced to the surrounding murmur of a babbling brook and a choir of birds. A light breeze swayed the willow tree branches, and the sweet aroma of flowers filled the air. Heinrick stood proudly watching Anna approach him. She was everything he had dreamed for a wife.

"I am proud of you," Tanya replied, then kissed Anna on her forehead.

Next, Tanya put Anna's hand into Heinrick's hand.

"I love you, Mama," Anna said, then turned to look into Heinrick's blue eyes. The pastor asked everyone to sit down then began reading from the Bible.

"Hurry up; we have a honeymoon to get to," Heinrick mouthed to Anna.

"Shhh," Anna mouthed.

Enchanted by their fairy-tale moments, Heinrick and Anna were unaware of their surroundings even after the pastor had introduced them.

"Ladies and Gentlemen, let me introduce you to Mr. and Mrs. Müller," The pastor announced.

" pssst, Time to go," The pastor whispered to Anna and Heinrick.

The pastor turned to the crowd.

"Congratulations!" The pastor yelled out then motioned the audience to do the same.

"Congratulations!" The crowd yelled.

Heinrick and Anna suddenly realized that they were being called to join in their celebration.

They looked at each other and laughed, then held hands and ran down the aisle while guests continued cheering them on. When Anna and Heinrick had reached the horse and carriage, six little girls stood on either side of the carriage giggling and throwing roses at them. Anna and Heinrick stepped into the carriage and the horses trotted down the cobblestone road to greet their guests and dance to their heart's content.

" It's time for the toasts," Randolph announced.

"Congratulations to Anna and Heinrick!" the crowd shouted.

"Wishing you lifelong happiness!" One guest yelled out.

"As they say in Armenian, 'shall you grow old on one pillow!'" The Armenian guest chimed in.

"Congratulations from Endelman!" the rebel said, then left the premises.

After the wedding, Anna donated the jewelry to the museum her father used to take her to. It now belonged to the people of Austria. She and Heinrick decided it was the appropriate time. Anna would be recounting its history, which was bound to bring more visitors and curiosity seekers to the museum.

CPSIA information can be obtained
at www.ICGtesting.com
Printed in the USA
LVHW071902031121
702365LV00024B/1124

9 781662 828614